A Haunted Disappearance

A LIN COFFIN

COZY MYSTERY

BOOK 2

J.A. WHITING

Formatting by Signifer Book Design

Proofreading by Donna Rich

To hear about new books and book sales, please sign up for my mailing list at: www.jawhitingbooks.com

For the loved ones who watch over us

CHAPTER 1

Carolin Coffin sat at a small round table with Mallory listening to her cousin Viv's band play their version of a country-pop song that had people in the audience of the Nantucket pub singing and clapping along. Viv's golden brown hair shimmered under the stage lights as she held the microphone and danced about as she sang. Carolin didn't know how Viv had so much stamina. Her cousin carried a few extra pounds on her five- foot-five-inch frame and never exercised, but she had just put on a two-hour show full of energy and high spirits that drew the audience along with every note.

The song ended and Carolin and Mallory finished their glasses of wine just as Viv's voice spoke through the amplifiers. "For our last song of the night, I'd like to call my cousin, Lin, up here to join me." Viv waved to Lin with a big grin.

The blood drained out of Lin's head and she felt the room start to spin. She shook her head vigorously with a frown painted on her face. She and Viv had been singing together on Viv's deck some evenings after dinner, but she was absolutely sure she was not ready to perform in front of people. Drops of sweat trickled down Lin's back. She made eye contact with Viv and mouthed "No."

The crowd applauded encouragement and Mallory smiled and nodded. "Go ahead, Lin. It'll be great."

Lin's heart sank. She was sure it would not be great. What she really wanted to do was to sneak out of the place on her hands and knees, but decided that trying to escape would make her look more of a fool than singing with Viv.

A tall guy with droopy eyes caused from imbibing a few drinks too many got up and moved to Lin's side, took her hands, and gently tugged her to her feet.

Lin sighed. Her feet felt like blocks of cement as she started for the stage thinking of all the ways she could kill her cousin after the show. One of the guys in the band hurried over with a second microphone and hooked it onto a stand. Lin's knees were shaking so badly she hoped that her legs might give out and she could avoid the performance by collapsing and being hauled away in an ambulance.

As Viv held her guitar and swung the strap over her head, she leaned close to Lin, who was shooting daggers out of her eyes at her cousin, and said, "Just like when we're on the deck."

Viv started to play the song that she and Lin had been practicing together and her band followed her lead. The song was a fast pop song that was popular on the radio, but the girls had slowed it down and turned into a sweet, soulful tune that pulled at the heart strings. Viv began to sing and Lin came in on the chorus. The cousins voices blended and harmonized together so beautifully that after three verses were sung and the last note was played, the crowd was on its feet whooping and hollering and clapping so loudly that Lin's ears buzzed. She turned to Viv with a sheepish smile, her cheeks flaming red. Viv bear-hugged her reluctant cousin and whispered in her ear. "After getting a reception like this, I won't be able to drag you off the stage." The two held hands and took a bow, Lin's long brown hair falling forward over her face.

Before breaking down the equipment and packing it up for the night, the band members, Lin, and Mallory stood near the bar and had a drink together. They chattered about the gig, the audience, Lin's performance, and town happenings. Lin caught a glimpse of her necklace sparkling in the mirror behind the bar and her hand went up to her neck. She clasped the gold pendant between her forefinger and thumb. The necklace was once owned by one her ancestors and it was found in Viv's storage shed hidden there centuries ago by Sebastian Coffin, an early settler of Nantucket.

The pendant was gold and in its center was a white-gold horseshoe which tilted slightly to one side. The same design could be seen built into the bricks on the chimneys of several old houses on the island and was intended to ward off witches and evil spells. Sebastian Coffin had the design constructed into his own chimney, but not to keep witches away ... he used the symbol to draw people who had been accused of witchcraft to his home where he and his wife provided them a safe place to stay and helped them integrate into island life.

Other things had been found in Viv's storage shed along with the necklace, art work done by a Renaissance painter and printmaker, gold coins, and maps thought to have belonged to a famous pirate whose loot had never been found and was estimated to be worth in the billions in today's dollars. Viv had turned the items over to an appraiser and had contacted a museum in Boston with the intention of donating the things so that the public could enjoy them. She had no desire to keep the things that had been given as gifts to Sebastian Coffin and his wife, Emily, for providing safe haven to the persecuted individuals. Viv had said that Sebastian and Emily Coffin didn't want to profit from the misfortune of others, and neither did she. Viv gave Emily Coffin's horseshoe necklace to Lin because her cousin and Emily shared a similar characteristic. Lin and Emily could both see ghosts.

When Viv announced the late hour and her need

to get to bed since she had an early morning the next day opening her book store and café, everyone agreed it was time to head home. Dave, one of the band members, went to get the equipment van and the others broke down the stage items and started carrying things outside to the sidewalk to load into the vehicle as soon as Dave had retrieved it from the small parking lot down the road.

The stars were shining in a clear, early July night sky. Despite how late it was, tourists still strolled along the brick sidewalks of Nantucket town under old-fashioned streetlights leaving restaurants after eating dinner, heading to pubs for a drink, window shopping, and walking down to the docks to view the boats and yachts moored there.

Lin hauled an amplifier out the door of the pub and when she stepped onto the brick walkway, the toe of her shoe caught on an uneven brick and she turned her ankle causing her to lose her balance. She waved her free arm in the air trying to maintain an upright stance, but her body's twisting motion along with the weight of the heavy piece of equipment caused her to tumble onto her butt and hit the sidewalk hard. Although the amplifier was undamaged, Lin couldn't say the same for her rear end. She leaned forward onto her knees and pushed herself up just as someone's hand slipped under her arm and gave her a boost to her feet.

Lin gave a pained smile to the person who helped her up as she rubbed her tailbone. "These brick sidewalks sure are hard."

"It's easy to trip on the bricks." A tall young man of about twenty with bright blue eyes smiled at Lin.

A pretty girl with long, dark brown hair and about the same age as the boy righted the amplifier. "The cobblestone streets are even worse. I'm always tripping over them." She smiled at Lin showing perfect rows of white teeth. "Maybe we're just klutzes."

Lin chuckled. "That's probably the reason."

Dave pulled up to the curb, jumped out, and opened the rear doors of the van. The young man carried the amplifier over to the vehicle and helped Dave load it into the back.

"You're sure you're okay?" The girl looked at Lin with concern.

"Oh, I'm fine." Lin nodded. "But I'm sure I won't be able to sit down tomorrow." She and the girl shared a laugh. Lin liked the young woman's easy-going, friendly personality.

Just then Viv lumbered through the door of the pub carrying two guitar cases. Lin hurried to help her, but Viv waved her off. "Could you grab the other case? It's just inside the door." She nodded her head towards the pub entrance and then shuffled to the van, her arms hanging straight down by her sides clutching the large cases. "Maybe someday we'll be famous and we can hire people to lug our equipment around."

Lin smiled and started to walk back inside to

grab the case that housed the microphones and electrical cords. Reaching for the door handle, a jolt of something shot through Lin's blood, a sensation of foreboding or anxiety, a feeling that something was wrong. She turned back to see the two young people helping Viv with the guitar cases. Lin shrugged and tried to shake off the odd sensation.

When she came back out, she carried the metal container to the van and handed it off to Dave. She glanced around for the young couple to thank them again for helping her when she fell, but she couldn't see them anywhere.

Viv hurried back inside the pub and came back out carrying her guitar case. "I'm ready to head home." She yawned and handed a backpack to her cousin. Lin slung it over her shoulder and couldn't keep a yawn of her own from slipping from her mouth. In the pleasant night air, the two headed up the road to Main Street and to their houses on the outskirts of town.

CHAPTER 2

Lin packed her lunch into her bag and added a cold pack before pressing on the Velcro to close it. She stepped out on the deck and called for her dog. Nicky bounded out from behind the trees at the rear of the property and rushed up the steps of the deck where he danced around wagging his stub of a tail. The little brown mixed-breed was a rescue animal and his cheerful, playful personality always made Lin grin.

"Come on, Nick. We need to get to work." Lin had recently moved back to Nantucket island, the place of her birth, and was running a gardening business where she mowed lawns, trimmed, and took care of her clients' flower gardens, window boxes, and pots of blooms. Lin had been a computer programmer in Cambridge, MA before moving and she still did part-time work for the company remotely. The two jobs provided enough to pay her bills and save a little each month. When the winter came and her gardening business slowed to a halt, Lin hoped to be able to pick up more programming hours.

As she and the dog walked to her old truck, she hummed the song that she and Viv had sung on stage last evening. She shook her head thinking about being pulled up in front of the crowd and even though it had turned out well, her heart pounded just recalling her terror of being in front of an audience. Sitting down in the driver's seat, her butt ached from having fallen on the brick sidewalk last night and she shifted her weight trying to find a more comfortable position. She started her truck, backed out, and headed off to her first client of the day who had recently contracted with Lin for her gardening services.

The morning air held the promise of a hot day and Lin hoped she could get her appointments finished before the late afternoon heat took hold. She turned the radio on and sang along enjoying the breeze streaming in through her open window. Nicky had his front paws on the armrest of the door and his nose pushed up to the three-inch window opening, sniffing the smells on the air.

After a ten-minute drive, Lin parked at the curb and hauled her equipment bag from the truck's bed. She and Nicky went to the front door and she rang the bell. Lin liked to alert the homeowners when she arrived to work so she wouldn't startle them when they saw someone moving about their yard and gardens. No one answered the bell, so Lin and her dog followed the walkway to the back of the house where small garden plots and pots on the deck were bursting with flowers and greenery.

When she'd started her job over a month ago, Lin returned home each night with sore and achy muscles, but now she was feeling stronger and better able to handle the outdoor work. She pulled a small bucket from the shed at the rear of the yard and began to deadhead the flowers. Lin hummed as she worked and the dog ran about the property with his nose to the ground. She had trained him never to dig or mess up the clients' yards and he never ran off the property where Lin was working.

She knelt and worked her way along the bed, pulling out weeds and plucking off faded blossoms. Lin had plans later in the day to meet Libby Hartnett for coffee at Viv's bookstore. Libby was a distant relative of Lin's on her mother's side of the Witchard family. Many of the Witchard women had paranormal powers and Libby had been meeting with Lin for the past few weeks to share family history with her. Libby couldn't see ghosts like Lin could, but she had the ability to transfer thoughts and images to someone just by holding their hand. Lin had grown up off-island and had never known anyone with powers until she'd arrived on Nantucket in early June and met Libby.

Lin stood and stretched her back and went to the side of the house where she unrolled the hose. The hot sun beat down on her shoulders as she worked from one end of the patio to the other watering the flower pots. She'd left her work bag on the deck near the sliding glass doors and needed a trowel, so she climbed the few steps and walked across the deck to the canvas bag.

She reached inside and removed the tool, and when she straightened, she could see a person inside the house reflected in the glass of the door. The figure looked just like the girl who had helped her last night. Thinking what a funny coincidence it was that the girl lived in the house of her newest client, she smiled and raised her hand to wave. Lin squinted and realized that the glass wasn't reflecting the image of the girl from inside the house. The girl was standing behind her.

In a split second, Lin noticed that the young woman's face looked oddly blank except for her eyes which seemed heavy and sad, such a contrast from the lively, friendly girl she'd met last night. As she was about to turn to greet the young woman, a cold breeze fluttered over Lin's skin causing her to shiver.

Nicky ran over and whined.

Lin stopped in mid-turn, sucked in a breath, and closed her eyes for a moment, afraid of what she was about to see. Her heart pounded like a sledgehammer. She turned slowly around and a gasp slipped from her throat.

The girl stood several yards from Lin, her physical form almost translucent. Her body seemed to waver in the sunlight. The girl's long hair was mussed. Purple bruises showed on her neck. A bit of frothy pink spittle dribbled from the corner of her mouth. Someone else might take a quick look at the girl and think she'd had too much to drink or was slightly ill or had bit her tongue causing the saliva mixed with blood to leak onto her lip, but Lin knew differently. Lin knew the girl was dead.

CHAPTER 3

Confusion shot through Lin's brain as she stared slack-jawed at the girl. Her first instinct was to rush to the girl and wrap her in her arms, but all the ghosts she'd met previously would shrink from physical interaction and, anyway, Lin assumed that there really wasn't much there to grasp on to. Nicky whined as Lin took a shaky step forward.

In a soft voice, she asked the girl, "What's happened?" As soon as the words were spoken, she realized how foolish they sounded.

The girl seemed to choke and her hand flew up to her throat. She leaned slightly forward, her chest rising and falling in quick succession as if she might heave. In a moment, she straightened and looked at Lin with such mournful eyes that Lin's heart lurched from an intense spasm of grief.

Lin took another step. "What can I....?"

The ghost's eyes shut momentarily and when she opened them they were filled with tears. Her image seemed to spark in places and then the form slowly began to fade.

"No." Lin reached out her hand. "Don't go."

The girl's body shimmered and disappeared.

Tears overflowed from Lin's eyes and she sank to the ground. Nicky crept over and Lin grasped him into her arms and rocked.

After several minutes, the dog gave Lin a lick on the cheek and she ran her hand over the animal's soft fur. "What happened to her, Nick? What happened?" Lin sucked in deep breaths and tried to collect herself. "Come on, boy." She stood, grabbed her tools and work bag and then she and the dog jogged to her truck. She loaded the things in the back and took her phone out of the bag. She tapped the screen to pull up the local news. When the stories of the day loaded, she flicked her finger over the screen scanning for an article or report about a young woman's murder. Nothing.

Lin jumped into the truck and pulled away from the curb with a screech, turning the vehicle towards town and Viv's bookstore. The truck bumped over the cobblestone streets and she spotted a parking space.

She and Nicky hurried into the bookstore and went directly to the back of the place where the café was located. Customers sat at the tables and on the comfortable sofas chatting and enjoying their early morning drinks and bakery items. Viv stood behind the café counter preparing an iced coffee when she noticed her cousin coming down the aisle. The look on Lin's face almost caused Viv to drop the glass she was holding. Her brow furrowed and she narrowed her eyes. She mouthed, "What's wrong?"

Libby Hartnett was sitting on a sofa with her usual morning chat group of two retired men and a woman. Sensing that something was wrong, Libby stared at Lin as she stepped around some of the customers waiting at the counter to place their orders.

Lin made eye contact with Viv and lowered her voice. "I need to talk to you."

Viv nodded and bustled about finishing the drinks she was making. As Lin turned away to locate a table at the edge of the café area, she saw Libby's eyes drilling into hers. Lin shrugged a shoulder and her lower lip started to quiver. She blinked hard to keep tears from falling.

Libby excused herself from the group and rushed over to Lin, put her arm around the young woman, and led her to a table where they both sat.

Libby leaned forward, her blazing blue eyes boring into Lin's. "What on Earth is wrong?" Her voice was barely above a whisper.

Lin glanced back to the counter to see Viv hurrying over. When Viv joined the two at the table, she reached over and placed her hand on her cousin's arm. "What is it? You look like you've seen a ghost." Viv realized what she'd just said and her eyes widened. "Oh." Her hand trembled. "*Have* you seen a ghost?"

Lin gave a slight nod.

Libby worried that Lin was about to lose her composure so she used an authoritative tone when she said, “Take a deep breath.” Libby decided to begin with simple questions to get Lin talking. “Where did you see the ghost?”

Lin told her.

“Was it Sebastian Coffin?”

“No.” Lin swallowed hard trying to clear away the emotion that held tight in her throat. She nervously fingered the gold pendant hanging around her neck.

“Did the ghost threaten you?”

Lin shook her head vigorously. “No.” She clutched her hands in her lap. “Have you heard anything about a murder on the island either last night or early this morning?”

Viv jerked back and the color drained from her face. “A murder?” Some people glanced over at Viv and she lowered her voice. “Someone was murdered?”

Lin told Libby and reminded Viv about the young couple who had helped last night after the gig when Lin fell on the sidewalk. “They were both so friendly and nice.”

“So? What do they have to do with a murder?” Viv eyed her cousin not really wanting to hear the answer.

“It was the girl. I was at a new client’s house working in the yard. The girl was behind me.”

Libby and Viv didn’t make the connection that

Lin was trying to get across.

"She's dead," Lin blurted. "The girl who helped me outside the club last night, it was her. She was standing behind me this morning. She's dead."

Viv's mouth dropped open in the shape of an "O" and her hand flew to her face. "Are you sure? Are you sure it was her? Are you sure she's dead?"

Lin looked at Viv. "I'm sure it's her." She squeezed her lips together and then said, "She's definitely dead."

"Did the ghost communicate with you?" Libby's facial muscles tensed.

"No. She just looked at me." Lin wrapped her arms around herself. "Her look ... it filled me with grief." Lin leaned against the chair back and touched her throat. "The girl's neck ... there were bruises, some blood was at the corner of her mouth." She put her hand back in her lap. "There isn't any news about a murder?"

Viv's face was pale. "I haven't heard a thing. People would be talking about it in here if a murder was reported on the news."

Libby's eyes darkened. "There's a reason why no one is talking about it. The body hasn't been found yet."

"What should I do?" Lin asked. "Go to the police?"

"Definitely not." Libby made eye contact with Lin. "How would you explain your knowledge that a young woman had been killed?" The older woman shook her head. “No. Hopefully, someone will discover the poor girl soon.”

Viv said, “Maybe she wasn’t murdered at all. Maybe it was an accident.”

“That’s not the feeling I got from her.” Lin thought for a minute. “What should I do if she comes back? Should I ask questions about her death? Does she even know she’s dead?”

“That can be tricky.” Libby tapped a finger on the table top. “You should project kindness and concern, but don’t press for answers. You can ask her what happened, but use a gentle tone. See if you get some form of communication from her. Assure the girl that you’d like to help.” Libby stood up. “I’m going to place a call to someone to ask her advice.” She hurried to the front of the store to make the call outside away from any possible eavesdroppers.

Viv turned to her cousin. “Are you okay?”

Lin nodded. “It was a shock. Most of the ghosts I’ve seen have been long dead. Someone so young....” She shook her head and let her comment trail off. “She was with a young man last night. I assumed it was her boyfriend.” Lin’s lips pressed together for a second. “I wonder if he....”

“Killed her?” Viv rubbed her forehead. “Oh, God.”

“I wonder if we could have done something to stop it. I should have paid closer attention to the way they interacted with each other.” Lin frowned.

"I remember thinking they made a nice couple. I didn't sense anything was wrong between them. They seemed to have an easy relationship. At least it seemed that way for the few minutes I spoke with them." Lin sat up straight, her eyes wide. "Wait. I *did* feel something was off. Right when I was going back inside the club to get the bag." She looked off across the room trying to recall the sensation she'd experienced. "I felt like something was wrong. A shot of anxiety went through me, but I just shrugged it off." Lin looked at Viv. "Was it foreshadowing what was to come?"

"Oh, my." Viv patted her chest. "How could you know what might happen? How would you know something bad was going to happen?"

Lin didn't have an answer. She had no idea. "Where's Libby?"

As if summoned, Libby came around the corner of one of the book shelves and sat down. "I spoke with a friend. She agrees that you should handle the ghost as we discussed. Be kind, gentle. My friend said that you may ask a few questions, but she suggests letting the spirit take the lead."

"Okay." Lin wasn't sure how to do that. She decided that if the girl returned, she would ask a few things and then see what happened. "You have a friend who can see ghosts?"

Libby gave the slightest of nods. "She's old. She doesn't accept visitors very often." The blonde woman gave Lin a pointed look. "I want you to meet her one of these days, but when that will happen is anyone's guess." Libby turned the palms of her hands up.

"I wonder how soon someone will find the body?" Viv saw Mallory gesturing to her to come back to the counter and help with the customers. Viv held up an index finger indicating she'd be there in a second.

"That depends where the body is." Libby had an angry expression on her face.

"Someone will miss her soon." Lin tried to be hopeful. "They'll call the police to report her missing and then they'll search for her."

Libby frowned. "That could take a while. The girl might be on-island for summer work. She might be staying in an employee group-house where a restaurant or store provides a place to live for some of the employees. There are usually a number of people residing in a house. It could be a while until someone notices her absence."

Viv said, "The people she lives with might assume she's staying with her boyfriend."

"But she'll miss her shift at work," Lin said. "That will alert someone."

Libby shrugged. "It depends on how soon her next shift is and, anyway, sometimes young people don't show up to work. It happens pretty frequently." Libby worked part-time in a high-end home goods store. "They don't call in and when they do show up for their next shift they say they were out sick. The boss will reprimand them, but it's hard to get summer workers so they don't often get fired." Libby checked her phone. "It could take a few days before anyone thinks to call the police."

Lin sighed. "I need to get back to work."

"Let us know if the young woman makes another visit." Libby stood and returned to her friends.

The cousins made plans to have dinner together at Viv's house. Leaving the bookstore, a shudder of helplessness ran down Lin's back and even though she wanted the girl's body to be found soon, she hoped that the ghost would move on and wouldn't come back to pay her a visit.

CHAPTER 4

The girls sat on Viv's deck sipping some wine before their dinner was ready. Nicky and Viv's cat, Queenie, lay side by side on the grass near the bottom of the steps sniffing the air and watching birds dart by and squirrels run up the trunks of trees.

When Lin returned to work after her visit to the bookstore to report the ghost's visit, she kept looking over her shoulder as she tended the flowers in her clients' gardens and she jumped at the slightest noise or the gentlest breeze afraid the ghost girl was about to make another appearance.

"Why would the ghost show herself to you?" Viv checked the time on her watch to be sure the dinner wasn't burning. "How would she know you were working in that particular yard?"

Lin scowled. "I have no idea. I only see ghosts. I don't know anything about them. They just show up."

"Why do they? What do they want when they show up?" Viv shifted in her seat, clearly uncomfortable with the subject.

Lin thought about the question. "When I was little, ghosts would stand at the end of my bed and watch me sleep or they'd stand off to the side while I played. I never asked them questions, except sometimes I asked their names."

"Did they speak to you?" Viv was fascinated and uneasy at the same time.

"I don't recall ever hearing a ghost's voice, not like I hear yours. It was always like a word just forming in my head." Lin made a face. "I think."

"What about when Sebastian was here?" Viv asked. "Did he ever speak to you?"

"No. I almost felt some communication from him now and then, but it wasn't a voice talking, it was more like me hearing words in my brain." Lin cocked her head. "That doesn't really make sense, I guess."

"It does." Viv pondered. "Maybe."

"I don't really know what they want or why they show up. I remember that a couple of times, one of the woman ghosts that I saw stroked my hair as I was falling asleep. I bet I reminded her of her own little girl."

Viv looked uncomfortable with the thought of a ghost touching her.

Lin rubbed at a knot in her back. "When I was working today, I pulled my phone out every few seconds to search for news. I kept checking over my shoulder expecting to see the ghost. Any little noise caused me to jump."

Viv sipped her wine. "I was doing the same, looking for any news or information that the body of a young woman had been found."

"What can we do? How can we find her? We don't know her name or her boyfriend's name. We don't know where they lived or if they were residents here or summer visitors. How can we figure it out?"

Viv blew out a long sigh. "There must be a way, but it will be like looking for a needle in a haystack."

Lin looked out over the yard. Mature shade trees stood here and there, several garden plots held flowers and vegetable plants, and the lawn was lush and green even with all the hot weather the area had recently been experiencing. Her eyes settled on the ell, an original structure to the antique Cape that jutted off the back of the house. It had been used as a storage room for the past fifty years and when Viv inherited the place she had every intention of cleaning it out, but never got around to it.

Lin, Viv, Libby Hartnett, and an island historian and author, Anton Wilson, had recently found a chest in the storage room that had been hidden there over two hundred years ago by the cousins' ancestor, Sebastian Coffin. Even though the treasure had been appraised to be worth just over half a million dollars, Viv was in the process of making arrangements to donate the artwork, coins, and jewelry to a Boston museum.

Lin smiled looking at the ell. "Are things finalized with the museum?"

"The lawyer said the paperwork will be ready at the end of the month. Then I'll sign the documents and the things will belong to the Museum of Fine Arts in Boston."

"Any regrets about not keeping the things or not selling them?" Lin was pretty sure she knew what the answer would be.

"Absolutely none." Viv shook her head. "Those things didn't belong to me. I want them in a place where people can see them, hear the story behind the items, and enjoy looking at them. Those things shouldn't be locked up in some collector's home. And I don't want to profit from them either."

"You're very generous." Lin gave her cousin a smile.

Viv gave a mock evil chuckle. "Not that generous. I kept the best things for myself." Some treasure maps and cryptograms were found in the chest that supposedly belonged to the notorious pirate, La Buse, whose buried treasure had never been found.

Lin smiled and raised an eyebrow. "Well, when you travel to distant lands to dig up the treasure, remember your poor cousin when you strike it rich."

"I won't have to remember you because you'll be standing right next to me with a shovel."

Lin laughed. “A fifty-fifty split of the treasure?”

“You bet.” Viv stood to go check on the chili-chicken bake. “I’ll have to give you half because you’re going to decipher those cryptograms we found in the chest and that will lead us to the treasure.”

“You might have a long wait. I have no idea how to figure those out.” Lin loved crossword puzzles and anagrams and could finish them faster than anyone that Viv had ever seen. Lin shook her head. “And by the time I *do* figure it all out, we’ll be too old to go and dig.”

Viv waved her hand in the air. “In the meantime, I’m going to have some of the documents framed so I can hang them in the living room.”

“I wish Sebastian would come back and visit me.” Lin stood up to follow Viv into the kitchen. “I wonder if he knows how to decipher those maps and clues.”

Nicky and Queenie knew the women were heading inside for the food so they raced up the steps and onto the deck. Lin let them in before she entered. “I wonder if Sebastian could help us figure out where the body of the girl is located.” In the kitchen, Viv opened the oven door and the spicy odor of the baking chicken filled the room. “If I recall correctly, Sebastian wasn’t exactly a talkative ghost. I doubt he would be able to give you any information.”

Lin took the dressing from the fridge and picked up the bowl of salad from the table. "Still, I wouldn't mind a visit." When Sebastian first showed up in Lin's house last month, she was shocked and frightened. She hadn't seen a ghost in over twenty years and the sight of the spirit brought up old feelings of rejection that had developed when she was nine years old when she shared her "ability" with someone she thought was a friend. The cruel girl turned on Lin and told other kids that Lin was weird and odd and lied about ghosts just to seem special. Having the last name of Coffin didn't help matters either and only added to the bullying and teasing that ensued.

Sebastian had made several appearances during the recent murder case that Lin and Viv were involved with and Lin had begun to welcome the visitations from the eighteenth-century ghost. She hadn't seen him for weeks and missed his unannounced arrivals.

Viv had cooked some chicken without the spice that she'd put on hers and Lin's pieces and she cut up the plain meat and put it on two plates that she carried out to the deck. She set the dishes down for the dog and cat and, with Nicky practically drooling, the animals hurried to gobble their meals.

Lin carried out a tray with condiments, the salad bowl, and a jug of iced tea. Viv went back inside and returned to the deck with two plates of chicken and rice which she set on the table. Lin lit some candles and the girls sat down to a delicious dinner. They wanted to talk about other things besides ghosts. Viv told Lin that her boyfriend John was having a great year so far with real estate sales picking up. She worried that he was working too much with his realty business and then gigging with their band several times a week.

Viv wiped her lips with her napkin. “John loves what he does. I just don’t want him to run himself into the ground.”

Lin agreed and then she told her cousin that Jeff, the man she’d been dating for the past few weeks, would be returning from the mainland in a few days. Lin met the attractive carpenter when she’d hired him to make a doggy door in her kitchen so Nicky could come and go as he wanted. Jeff had been working on a job outside of Boston and the work was almost complete. Lin couldn’t wait for him to return to Nantucket. The two had hit it off right away and they’d been enjoying each other’s company with nice dinners on Lin’s deck, bike rides, and trips to the beach.

Lin sipped her iced tea and looked at the soothing greenery all around them. The sun was sinking behind the trees at the back of Viv’s yard and was painting streaks of rose, violet, and gold across the sky. Lin smiled thinking about how lucky she was to have inherited her grandfather’s house, to have a growing business and a new boyfriend, and to be back on the island with her cousin and best friend. She couldn't remember ever being as happy as she was now.

Reaching for her glass, Lin's hand stopped in mid-air. Her heart squeezed with a jolt of sadness when her thoughts returned to the young woman she'd met last night. She let out a long sigh, thinking about the unfairness of life.

Lin told Viv how she was just counting her blessings when her mind flickered back to the image of the ghost-girl. "It's so hard to believe that I can sit here eating a delicious meal and chatting with my best friend and that poor girl's body is out there undiscovered." Lin leaned back against her chair. "What could have happened to her? She seemed so happy last night." She shook her head slowly. "Things can change in an instant, can't they?'

Viv placed her fork on her plate. "They sure can." A dark expression formed across her face. "Do you think her boyfriend killed her? Or was it a random attack? She could have run into some nut on her way home."

Lin gave a shrug of her shoulder. "I wish we could find out who she was, who the boyfriend is. At least that would be a start. Right now we have absolutely nothing to go on."

"Zero." Viv nodded. "Wouldn't it be nice to be able to go back in time? Then we could warn her. Of what, I don't know, but we could tell her to be on guard."

A sad smile played over Lin's lips and then she sat up straight, her blue eyes wide. "Wait. What if...." Her voice carried a tone of excitement. "What if she *isn't* dead?"

CHAPTER 5

Confusion furrowed Viv's brow.

"What if what I saw was a premonition?" Lin leaned forward. "What if what I saw was a *possibility*, but wasn't yet reality? Is the future fixed, predetermined? Or is what I saw a warning of what *might be,* what *could be*, if things aren't altered?"

Viv sat across from her cousin with her mouth hanging open. "Huh?"

"Maybe," Lin told her cousin, "she's alive. Maybe it wasn't a ghost at all that visited me. What if it was a vision of what might happen?"

Viv ignored her mug of iced tea and reached for her wine glass. She took a long sip and then stared across the table at Lin. "So now you have a new skill? You don't just see ghosts anymore. You can see the future?"

"I'm just guessing."

"I think you're being hopeful." Viv crossed her arms and leaned on the table. "I think you're desperate to make things better, to make whatever happened to this girl disappear."

"You think I'm clutching at something that isn't possible?"

"Have you ever sensed a future event?" Viv addressed her cousin with a serious expression. "When you were little? Were you ever able to see the future, even in some minor way?"

The hint of a frown pulled at Lin's lips. "No." Her hand moved to her horseshoe necklace and she worried it with her fingers. "But if I can see ghosts, who's to say I can't develop other abilities?"

"It seems convenient." Viv looked skeptical. "Because you want this girl to still be alive." She tapped her finger on her chin. "Did anything about today's visitation seem different from any other ghostly appearance you've experienced?"

Lin didn't answer. She replayed the morning's visit in her mind trying to notice or remember anything at all that seemed different than the times other ghosts had appeared to her. "I felt upset. Other times I've felt surprised, or annoyed, and a couple of times frightened, but never as upset as I was this morning."

"That could just be because you had met the girl the night before or because it was a young person or that it was so unexpected to see her like that."

"I guess," Lin admitted.

The candlelight shimmered over Viv's face making her eyes look all sparkly. "After dinner, why don't we walk around town, see if we can find the girl or her boyfriend. Maybe we'll bump into one of them."

"Okay. That's a good idea." Lin looked her cousin in the eye. "You don't think it was a premonition, do you?"

"It could be. It would be wonderful if that's what it was."

"But?" Lin cocked her head.

Viv's eyes softened. "But I think it's unlikely."

The girls cleared the table and went in to clean up and load the dishwasher. They brought the dog and cat inside and then they locked the doors and headed for the sidewalk.

"A walk will do me good." Viv opened the white picket fence gate and the girls stepped off of the stone walkway and onto the brick sidewalk that would lead into town. The closer they got to town, the more people filled the sidewalks. "Let's head down to the pub where we played last night. Maybe the girl and her boyfriend live near there. Maybe they're in that section of town a lot and we'll run into them."

"You're pretty smart, you know." Lin winked.

"I know," Viv grinned. "Just call me Einstein."

When they reached the sidewalk in front of the pub, Viv stopped and glanced around. She saw a security camera attached to the wall of the building up high near the roof. She touched Lin's arm and pointed.

"What?" Lin squinted. "What good is a security

camera? The murder, if one was committed, didn't happen here in front of the pub." She was still grasping at the possibility that what she'd seen that morning had been a premonition.

"John is good friends with the owner." Viv smiled. "He could ask for access to the film. If the camera caught the girl and her boyfriend on tape, then we could print off the still pictures of their faces and use the photographs to ask around about them."

Lin's eyes went wide. "You really are a genius." She hugged her cousin. "Call John. Ask him to call the owner."

Viv held up her phone. "I'm on it."

Viv made the call and even though she hated to fib to John, she couldn't give him the real reason that she and Lin wanted the still photographs. She made up a story that Lin had found the girl's necklace on the ground. It looked extremely valuable and she wanted to try to find her so that she could return it to her. John agreed to call his friend and make the request.

Lin and Viv linked arms and strolled down the street. If the pub owner was able to get a photograph from the security video, it wouldn't be ready that night. They decided to walk around town with an eye out for the girl's boyfriend.

"Did you notice which way the couple went last night after they helped us?" Viv asked.

"I didn't even see them leave." Lin shook her head. "I went in to get the bag and when I came back out, they were gone. I did glance around because I wanted to thank them again for their help, but I didn't see either one."

Viv's phone buzzed and she took the call from John. When she clicked off, she turned to her cousin. "John says the pub owner has been going through the security tape. The pictures aren't ready, but he thinks he recognizes the young man who helped you up last night. He said he thinks the guy works at the Irish pub a few blocks down the street from here."

"That's great. Let's go." Lin tugged on Viv's arm.

"Do you want to wait until tomorrow when we get the pictures?"

"If the guy isn't working, we can describe him to some of the staff." Lin was excited to have a lead in finding out the identity of the two people. "Let's go see what they say."

The girls hurried down the streets to the Irish pub and went inside. The place was packed with customers and loud music played over the speakers. Blonde wood lined the walls and the floor was gleaming wide pine. Lin had to lean close to Viv in order to be heard. "Where should we start?"

The hostess came up to the girls. "There's about a forty-minute wait. Would you like to give your name?"

Lin shook her head. "No, thanks. We're actually looking for someone who works here. About five foot nine, blonde sandy hair, cut short with longer bangs. He's in his early twenties."

The hostess gave Lin a suspicious look and didn't respond.

"He isn't in any trouble." Lin thought it best to assure the young woman of that. "He helped us with something. We'd like to give him a reward."

"I don't know who you're asking about." The hostess still had a wary look on her face.

"Is there someone here who meets our description?" Viv took a step forward. "We were told he works here."

"Not really. I don't know who you mean."

"Can we speak with the manager?" Lin smiled being careful not to be aggressive or confrontational in her tone.

The hostess gave a slight snort and walked through the dining room to the bar.

"Why is she being so suspicious?" Viv watched the woman speaking to a tall, black-haired man who glanced in the girls' direction. The man headed towards them.

"I'm the manager. Can I help you?"

Viv explained what they wanted.

"Nobody is working here who meets that description." The manager wasn't exactly cordial and his bearing and clipped response made Lin decide that she would never want to eat at this establishment.

"Did anyone ever work here that meets that description?" Viv eyed the guy.

"I suppose over the years that someone may have." He put his hands in his pockets. "I need to get back to work. Sorry I couldn't help." The guy strode away in the direction of the bar.

The girls stepped out of the noise of the restaurant and into the relative quiet of the busy sidewalk.

Lin pulled on her earlobe. "I think I've lost some of my hearing from being in there."

"What's wrong with them?" Viv's forehead scrunched in anger. "I would describe that interaction as bordering on rude. Couldn't that guy just say something like it was against restaurant policy to give out information on employees? He made me feel like I was doing something wrong." She stomped her feet as she walked along.

"I guess they don't want to share anything about their employees." Lin scurried along to keep up with Viv. "Or he's hiding something."

Viv stopped in her tracks and stared at Lin. "Could that guy be involved in the girl's disappearance?"

Lin swallowed hard. "I didn't think of that. What's going on?" She glanced back over her shoulder towards the restaurant and a nervous shiver rolled through her stomach.

CHAPTER 6

Lin woke earlier than usual and pulled out her phone to check the news. There was still nothing reported about the death of a young woman. As she was making breakfast, Nicky ran in through the doggy door and tore around the kitchen. Lin shook her head at the crazy dog. He was great company and his antics always made her happy. "What's got into you this morning?"

The dog halted, looked up at Lin, woofed and shot into the living room, his tiny stub of a tail wagging back and forth as he ran. Lin laughed as she tipped the frying pan and pushed the scrambled eggs onto her plate. She bent and placed some of the eggs into the dog's dish. When he heard the scrape of the spatula in the pan, Nicky lurched out of the living room and back into the kitchen to his dish. He wolfed down the eggs before heading off with his owner for her workday.

Lin spent hours in the hot sun working in her client's gardens and looking over her shoulder for ghosts. Leonard Reed, a landscaper Lin had met during a recent case that she and Viv had been involved in, worked side by side with the young woman for over an hour at one client's yard lifting and re-positioning patio stones that had heaved up during the cold winter. Leonard was lacking in social graces, sometimes got into trouble with the local police due to minor offenses, and often went without a shower for several days which could make it difficult to work with him. Lin had misjudged the man last month thinking that he was a murderer and she'd been sorry for jumping to conclusions about him. Leonard had been stabbed when trying to warn Lin about a suspect and she got to know him over the course of several visits to him in the hospital.

Leonard did good work and the company where he'd been previously employed was in the process of being sold, so Lin called him in to help her on jobs or suggested his name to clients whenever a job required more extensive labor or landscaping. She'd even started to enjoy Leonard's bawdy sense of humor.

After the long day of hard work, Lin took a shower and had a bite to eat, and then she and Nicky walked up Vestry Road, turned left, and followed the brick sidewalks into town. While Lin had been pulling weeds in a client's garden, she'd received a text from Viv reporting that John had delivered the photos from the security tape. He'd dropped them off at the bookstore during his lunch break. Lin was eager to see what the photos showed.

Lin and Nicky walked down the aisle of Viv's bookstore to the café section. Viv waved and indicated she'd be a few minutes. Libby and Anton Wilson, the island historian, sat at a table hunched over some paperwork. Viv's gray cat, Queenie, was perched on one of the upholstered chairs and Nicky jumped up beside her, gave her a lick on the ear, and settled next to the furry animal. Queenie gave the impression that she was only tolerating the little dog, but Lin thought the regal feline secretly enjoyed his company.

Viv wiped her hands on her apron and hurried over to Lin carrying a manila envelope. "Here they are. I didn't want to look at the photos on my own. I waited for you." She placed the envelope on the table and the girls sat. Viv slid it over in front of her cousin and Lin moved her hand gingerly to open the flap. She removed four black and white, grainy photographs and spread them over the table top. Her heart skipped a beat when she saw the young man and woman in the pictures. One photograph showed the girl facing the camera and smiling broadly at Lin.

Lin let out a sigh. "This is a good one of the girl." She handed it to Viv. "And this one is a good shot of the guy. It's fuzzy, but you can see his face well-enough."

Viv nodded. "We can use these." She looked at

her cousin. "You want to go down to the Irish restaurant tonight and ask around?"

"I think that's the best way to attack this." Lin was dreading having to approach the waitstaff as they got off work at the pub to show them the photos of the girl and guy. She didn't want the restaurant manager to harass them so they would need to be careful when they tried to talk to people.

Libby and Anton came over to the girls' table and Viv placed the envelope over the photos to hide them.

"It's okay," Libby said. "I've informed Anton of what's going on."

Viv removed the envelope and showed the photographs to Libby and Anton. Lin told them how they'd been able to obtain the shots.

Libby frowned. "I don't recognize either one of them. Do you, Anton?"

"I try to avoid young people." The wiry man bent to look closely at the pictures. "Most likely I wouldn't recognize them even if I had seen them. All young people look alike to me."

Libby rolled her eyes. "Really? Perhaps you need your eyeglass prescription adjusted."

Lin couldn't help a tiny grin forming.

Anton straightened. "It isn't my glasses. I don't pay attention to anyone younger than middle-age." He glanced at Viv and Lin. "Oh. Well. Present company excluded, of course."

"Of course." Lin smiled at the man.

"Any more sightings of the young woman?" Libby asked Lin.

"Nothing." Lin was glad that she was unable to report any more ghostly visits.

"A body hasn't been discovered yet either." Libby frowned. "Keep us informed." She and Anton headed out of the bookstore.

Viv got up and made sure her bookstore staff was set for the evening shift and then she and Lin collected the dog and cat. They walked up Main Street and turned right into Viv's neighborhood where they continued a few blocks to her Cape-style house. The girls warmed leftovers and ate out on the deck. They needed to wait until after midnight to stand outside the Irish restaurant waiting for employees to get off their shift, so the girls took short naps, Viv did some paperwork for her store, and Lin organized the next day's client list and texted Leonard about meeting her tomorrow to continue the patio stone work.

"I never expected you and Leonard to become friends." Viv didn't look up from her laptop.

Lin shrugged. "I wouldn't exactly call us friends. Business associates, I guess. But I'm glad I'm getting to know Leonard better. He hasn't had an easy life." She glanced at the clock. "Time to get going?"

Viv closed down her laptop and picked up the envelope containing the photos. "Let's go."

***

VIV SHIFTED from foot to foot. The girls had been standing on the sidewalk around the corner from the restaurant near the employee entrance for over an hour. Lin had on a baseball cap to pull down over her eyes if the manager came outside. Viv had a scarf over her hair and had removed her contact lenses and put on her glasses to try to disguise her appearance as best she could. "God, when do these employees go home? I could curl up on the bricks and fall asleep."

The side door opened and two young women and a man stepped out and headed towards the cousins.

"Here come some people." Lin opened the envelope and removed two of the photos.

Viv positioned herself in the middle of the sidewalk. "Hey. Could you take a look at these?" She pointed to the pictures in Lin's hand. "We're trying to find someone and wondered if you might recognize the people in these photos?"

Lin held them out for the three people to look at. They shook their heads and moved away. A few others left the building and the girls repeated their spiel. Again, the replies were negative.

"Maybe the guy never worked here at all." Viv sighed. "Maybe we got wrong information."

They tried two more employees with the same result. Lin held the photos up close to her eyes. "Is it too hard to make out the pictures? Is that why everyone says they don't recognize either of them?"

"Maybe people just don't care. They might be afraid of what we want, so they don't even try." Viv wrapped her arms around herself and yawned. "I need to call it a night. I have an early morning tomorrow. Make that today, since it is way after midnight. Come on, detective, let's go." She tugged on Lin's arm and they started back to Main Street walking in the dim light of the streetlamps. Lin couldn't suppress a yawn.

Just as they turned onto Main Street, someone spoke from close behind them. "Hey."

Viv almost jumped out of her skin. The girls stopped and whirled around.

"I saw your photos." A tall young woman with dark brown hair falling around her shoulders pushed her hands into the pockets of her loose sweater. "I just left the restaurant. I was with someone else so I didn't want to talk to you." She nodded to the envelope in Viv's hands. "I know them."

"You work in the restaurant?" Lin asked. She was afraid to get her hopes up.

The girl nodded. "I make the desserts."

"How do you know the guy in the picture?" Lin's heart was pounding.

"He worked at the restaurant for a while. Not long, maybe three weeks." The dark-haired woman looked over her shoulder.

"He quit?" Lin was doing all the asking. Viv

stood slightly behind her with a worried look on her face.

"No, he went back to work at another restaurant. Employees get shifted around between establishments sometimes. The same people own a bunch of restaurants around here."

"How long ago did he stop working at the pub?"

"About a week." The girl pushed her bangs across her forehead. "Why are you looking for him?"

Lin took a picture out of the envelope. "He helped me the other night. I fell and he helped me up, made sure I was okay. I wanted to give him a reward." She showed the picture to the woman, angling the photo in order to catch the light of the streetlamp. "You know the girl he's with?"

"Yeah." The dark-haired young woman took a look. "Yeah, she works at the pub." She glanced around the streets at the people walking by. "I better get going." She started to back away.

"What's the guy's name?" Lin had more questions and wished the woman wouldn't head off so quickly.

"Brian." The woman's brow creased in thought. She spoke as she was backing away. "I think his last name was something like Murphy, or Morton, or something like that. The girl's name is Amanda. I don't know her last name."

"Do you know where Brian lives?" Lin took a step forward.

"He said he lived over on Ellis Street. There are some places over there where seasonal workers live. Sorry I don't know more." She turned with her head down and walked briskly away.

"Thanks." Lin called after her. She looked at Viv. "Ellis Street."

"Not now?" Viv's eyes were like saucers.

Lin shook her head. "Tomorrow."

"She seemed kind of nervous," Viv said as they continued up Main Street. "It made me nervous."

"She kept looking around like she didn't want anyone to see her talking to us." Lin felt chilled and wished she'd brought a sweater.

"Why didn't she just talk to us when she came out of the restaurant with the other employee? Why did she have to speak to us privately?"

"I was wondering the same thing." Lin glanced back from where they had come.

"Why couldn't she speak freely in front of the other employee?" Viv scowled. "What's to hide? Why doesn't she want to be associated with the guy and girl in the photos? It sort of gives me the willies. Her behavior makes me nervous."

Lin agreed with her cousin.

Something just didn't seem right.

CHAPTER 7

Lin stopped at Viv's to get the dog and they headed home. It was much later than she expected to get back and she dreaded the early morning alarm. All the way back from Viv's place, she thought about the restaurant worker who had come up to them after they were out of sight of the establishment. Why couldn't the woman speak about the young people in the photos in front of others? The thought that the woman would only answer their questions in private caused a shiver to run over Lin's arms.

As she and the dog entered the bedroom, she rubbed her hands over her skin. Lin pulled on her sleep shorts and tank top and sat on the bed, reaching for her puzzle book. She decided to work on a crossword since she was too keyed up to fall asleep right away. She looked on the bedside table for the pen she kept with the book, but didn't see it so she leaned over the edge of the bed to see if it had fallen to the floor.

Lin sighed when she couldn't find the pen. She

placed the book on the bed and went to the kitchen to get another one. She heard Nicky whine and when she entered the living room, he was sitting on the sofa.

"What's wrong with you, Nick?" She scratched the dog's ears. "Did you think I left the house? I'm right here. Come on." She led the dog back into the bedroom where she pushed the pillows up against the headboard and settled down to work on the crossword puzzle for a while. She looked at the spot where she'd placed the book, but it wasn't there, so she lifted the blanket to see if it was under the covers. Not finding it, she looked over to the side table. The puzzle book was back on the bedside stand.

Goosebumps formed up and down Lin's arms. She flicked her eyes around the room without moving her head. *How did the book get off the bed? Is that why Nicky was whining?*

A month ago the ghost of Sebastian Coffin had moved a book from her living room to the deck table and she wondered if he might be back. If there was a ghost in the house, she hoped it was the eighteenth-century spirit and not someone different.

"Sebastian?" Lin whispered the name and waited for the tell-tale chill that enveloped her whenever a spirit was close by. No one materialized and the temperature in the room remained constant. A shiver of unease ran down her back.

Lin looked at the little dog sitting next to the bed. "You want to come up, Nick?" She patted the blanket. The dog jumped up and curled next to his owner. Lin was very happy to have the friendly creature's company. She turned off the light and hunkered down under the covers.

Shortly after falling asleep, Lin woke with a start and sat bolt upright. The room was freezing and she thought the air conditioning unit must have malfunctioned. Just as she was about to swing her legs over the side of the bed, she realized that the AC unit wasn't even running. She reached out her hand to feel for Nicky in the darkness patting the mattress in different spots without touching the dog. She heard him whine from the floor at the foot of the bed and she swallowed hard.

A flickering essence floated on the air in front of the bedroom window. Lin squinted and her heart pounded as the shimmering light took form. Lin's breath caught in her throat and the ghost girl, her body translucent, stood staring at Lin from the foot of the bed. Lin's mind raced. *What did Libby say? Be gentle with the ghost.*

The bruises on the girl's throat seemed to be lessening. Lin blinked and was about to ask if she was okay, but stopped herself before she could utter a word. *What a ridiculous question. Of course she's not okay.*

"You're Amanda?"

The girl stared. She didn't make a sound.

"How can I help?" Lin stayed sitting on the bed. She was afraid that movement might frighten the ghost away. "Do you know what happened?"

The girl looked down at her body. She lifted her hand and gazed for a few moments at her shimmery palm. She looked back at Lin. A glistening tear rolled down her cheek and she disappeared.

***

LIN DIDN'T sleep for the rest of the night. She and Nicky were sitting on the steps of the bookstore in the morning when Viv and Queenie came down Main Street to open up for the day. The cat walked alongside her owner like a dog.

When Viv saw them waiting, her face changed from a calm, pleasant expression to one of worry.

"What's happened?" Her voice quivered as she took out the key to the bookstore. Queenie and the little brown dog touched noses. Lin stood and told her cousin about the late night visit.

Viv's hand flew to her throat. "Oh." Her face clouded. "Why hasn't anyone found that poor girl's body?" She opened the door and flicked on the lights and the four of them went inside. Viv led the way down the middle aisle to the back of the store. She stepped behind the café counter where she busied herself with the morning tasks. "Where could that body be? It must be hidden. Who would kill her? Why would someone kill her? Why is this happening? How can there be another murder in town so soon?"

Lin sat on one of the counter stools. She was dressed for her gardening work in a pair of shorts and a dark tank top. Her long brown hair was pulled up into a ponytail. She had a slight grin on her face. When feeling nervous or upset, Viv sometimes rattled on and on about things.

Viv stopped what she was doing and put her hands on her hips. "Why are you smiling? None of this is amusing."

"Well, there's nothing amusing about this case, but there is something amusing right in front of me."

Viv batted the air with her hand. "I know that I'm going on about everything. It's just all terrible and I feel helpless."

"That's why I'm going to Ellis Street before my gardening jobs."

"I can't go. I can't leave the store."

"I know. I came to get one of the pictures. I'll go over there and ask around."

"Don't go alone. Wait for me. We'll go later." Viv poured water into one of the coffee makers.

"I feel like I have to go now."

Viv turned and eyed her cousin. "Why?"

Lin shrugged. "I don't know why. But I feel like it can't wait until later."

"What are you going to do?" Viv wrung her hands.

"Just ask around, show people the picture. Ask if anyone knows the two people in the photograph." A cloud passed over Lin's face. "We have to find out where this Brian guy is and what he's been up to." She leaned forward and whispered even though there wasn't anyone else in the store. "I've never seen a ghost in distress like this before. I need to help her, Viv."

Viv pressed her lips together and wrung the dish towel in her hands.

"There's nothing to worry about. It's broad daylight." Lin gave her cousin a smile.

"Danger doesn't care what time of day it is." Viv placed the towel next to the sink.

"I'll be okay." Lin got up from the stool. "Are the pictures in your office?"

Viv gave a little nod. "Please don't end up dead in a ditch somewhere. I couldn't take it." She saw Nicky sitting next to Queenie on the chair. "Leave the dog here. I need his company."

Lin headed for the bookstore's office to get one of the pictures. "I'll text you to report on my progress." After retrieving what she wanted from the manila envelope on Viv's desk, she left the store determined to find out something about the young man in the photo.

CHAPTER 8

Standing on the corner of Ellis Street and Holbrook Lane, Lin looked at the houses lining the road. Most were large, old homes that had been divided into apartments. The photograph taken from the security camera sat in her shoulder bag. She had no idea why she'd had the nagging notion to come to this neighborhood so early. She didn't know which house was the one where Brian Somebody might live and she wasn't sure what would happen when she found him. Lin only knew that every time she thought of the ghost girl, her heart contracted. She had to do something to help her.

Lin spotted a young man come through the front door of a house four doors up from where she was standing. She looked down to get the photo from her bag so she could ask him if he recognized the two young people in the picture. Her hand froze and she jerked her head up. There was something familiar in the way the guy held his body. He moved up the street at a quick pace and turned left heading for the next block. Lin hurried after him, picking up on a sense of urgency in the young man's step.

She followed him into the center of town where he turned right and walked several blocks heading towards the police station. Lin was only about ten yards from the man. Taking a chance, she called to him. "Brian?"

The young guy stopped and turned. He looked at Lin with quizzical eyes and then recognition passed over his face. "Oh. You fell the other night, right?"

Lin couldn't believe her luck.

The man looked different from the first time Lin had seen him. He almost seemed thinner, but she knew that wasn't possible in only three days. His face appeared haggard and pale and his shoulders drooped.

"I thought it was you." Lin extended her hand. "Lin Coffin."

"Brian Murphy."

"Thanks again for helping me the other night. I appreciate it."

"No problem." The guy took a step backward.

"Are you going to the police station?"

"What? Yeah."

Lin stepped forward. Her heart was pounding. "Is anything wrong?"

The guy shook his head, but his face betrayed his feelings.

"I've been looking for the girl you were with."

Lin held out the photo and the guy's eyes widened.

"Where'd you get that?" Brian looked like he might run off.

Lin ignored his question. "Do you know where I can find your friend?"

"No."

Lin cocked her head. "Have you seen her since the other night?"

Brian started to blubber something, but stopped. His eyes darted around. His breathing rate seemed to increase.

Lin stepped closer. "What's wrong?"

The young man's face started to crumble. "I ... I...."

Lin touched his arm. "You want to go sit down?" She gestured to one of the benches placed along the street. "Talk for a minute?"

Brian nodded and they went to the closest bench and sat.

"What's your friend's name?" Lin asked even though she knew what the girl's name was.

"Amanda." He coughed trying to clear his throat. "Amanda Robinson. She's my girlfriend."

"I wanted to give you and Amanda a small gift for helping me. I wanted to give you a gift card for dinner at your favorite restaurant." Lin smiled and then nodded sympathetically hoping to encourage Brian to tell what was troubling him.

Brian blinked a few times, but he didn't say anything so Lin asked, "What's wrong? Have you two broken up?"

Brian ran his hand through his short hair and hunched over clasping his hands between his legs. He stared at the ground. "We had a stupid fight. Right after we left you. It wasn't about anything, really, it was just one of those stupid fights that starts over nothing." He blew out a long breath. "She got mad at me over some dumb comment I made and she stormed away. I went after her, but she told me to go home. I always walk her back to the house she's staying in, but she told me to leave her alone, so I did what she asked. I was annoyed with her. I went home and left her alone."

Lin was trying to get a sense of the young man and if he was being sincere or was trying to cover over something he'd done. "You haven't talked to her since?"

Brian shook his head. "I've been texting her and calling her. She won't answer. I went to her house. The roommates said they haven't seen her. They thought she was with me. That's why I'm going to the police."

Lin bit her lip. This guy was either honestly concerned or he was a master liar. "Was Amanda involved in anything that might have caused her harm?"

Brian looked blankly at Lin.

"Drugs?"

"No. Never."

"Had she," Lin wasn't sure if she should add

what she was thinking, but then said, "or *you* been in trouble with anyone? Ever have a fight with anyone? Rubbed someone the wrong way?"

"No. We get along with everyone."

A flicker of unease washed over Lin. "Can you tell me a little about Amanda? How do you know each other? Are you students?"

Brian glanced over to the police station. Lin was afraid he would leave before she could find out about the girl.

"I'm only asking because I work as a gardener. I see lots of people each day. I could ask around, find out if anyone has seen her. It might help to locate her." Lin's heart sank, knowing that the young woman wouldn't be found alive.

"We go to Boston College. We're seniors. We've been dating since high school."

"What about her family?"

"She only has her dad, her mom died about six months ago. Her dad is a big executive at a company in Chicago, the CEO. We came to the island for the summer. Amanda worked at the Irish restaurant over on Green Street."

A shiver ran over Lin's skin. "Did you work there, too?"

"Only for a couple of weeks. I filled in for someone. I work at another restaurant, *The Golden Coin*, it's on Atlantic Ave."

"Did Amanda have trouble with anyone at the restaurant?"

"No. She never said anything like that." Brian sucked in a deep breath. He looked at Lin with big eyes. "Maybe she left the island and went home to Chicago. Maybe there's nothing to worry about."

"Did you call her at home in Chicago? Did you try her house?"

"I only ever call her cell phone."

"Has she ever gone off before? Has she gotten angry with you and didn't speak with you for a few days?" Lin wondered if there might be a friend that Amanda turned to when she was upset and if that friend might have had something to do with her death.

"We get annoyed with each other sometimes. She's never stopped talking to me though."

Lin pressed. "Is there anyone she confides in or hangs out with? Someone she might stay with if she was upset?"

Brian shrugged a shoulder. "I can't think of anyone. There's no one here on Nantucket anyway."

"Have you gone over to the Irish restaurant? Asked them when Amanda last worked?" Lin was trying to see how Brian would handle some questions. She couldn't get a handle on his guilt or innocence.

Brian shook his head. "I thought I'd better let the police handle it."

"I think you're right." Lin nodded. "Could we exchange phone numbers in case I hear something about Amanda or if you find out anything?" She and Brian traded contact information. They stood.

Lin's blue eyes were heavy with sadness. She wanted to say something positive to the young man, but didn't want to convey false hope. "The police will help."

Brian took a step towards the station. "I'll let you know as soon as she's found."

Lin smiled, but her face was devoid of emotion since the smile was forced. "I'd appreciate it." She watched Brian head up the stairs of the Nantucket Police Headquarters, and then she turned away with a heavy sigh.

CHAPTER 9

Lin drove along the road towards 'Sconset with Nicky standing on the arm rest of the passenger seat sniffing the air that came in through the top of the window. Leonard's truck had broken down and Lin told him she'd pick him up. One of the gardening clients wanted a stone patio put down and Lin had suggested Leonard's name and after showing photos of some of his work, the client hired Lin and Leonard to do the stonework.

After talking with Brian Murphy, Lin had hurried to the bookstore to pick up Nicky and to tell Viv what had gone on. The girls decided to pay a visit to the Irish restaurant later that evening to talk to some employees about Amanda Robinson.

Lin watched the road signs for the side lane that Leonard told her to turn onto. She shook her head and smiled at the way things had changed between her and the older landscaper. Seeing Rose Lane, Lin turned the truck down a narrow, tree-lined street of small Capes and ranches.

When she spotted the right house number, her

eyes widened and she pulled to the curb next to the white picket fence. She got out and stared at the flower gardens lining the inside of the fenced area at the front of the house. The small, gray-shingled Cape had the traditional crushed white shell driveway. White shutters hugged the sides of the windows and blue, white, pink, and yellow flowers spilled from the window boxes. A wide trellis stood next to the front of the house and lay across the roof. What looked to be thousands of pink roses climbed up the trellis and bloomed over the roof of the little Cape Cod-style home. Lin stood in front of the fence with her jaw hanging open.

Leonard stepped from the front door and came down the steps with a lunch box in his hand. "Mornin.'" He gave Lin a look. "What's wrong with you?"

Lin blinked at the gruff man. "This is the prettiest house I have ever seen."

Leonard nearly blushed. He grinned showing his missing and broken teeth. "I've had the place a long time, been working on it for years."

"Well," Lin smiled. "It's gorgeous." She glanced at the carefully chosen flowers and greenery and looked back at Leonard as he opened the gate and stepped out of his front yard. "Is your wife a gardener, too? Is she home?" Working together the past few weeks, Lin had noticed a simple gold band on Leonard's left ring finger, but he'd never mentioned his wife.

A look of surprise crossed Leonard's face. "She died a long time ago."

"Oh, I'm sorry. I saw your wedding ring and thought...."

"It's okay. I'm still married as far as I'm concerned. I love her."

Lin stared at Leonard's face. She was amazed that the older man was still so devoted to his late wife. "You know what? You're full of surprises." She smiled.

Leonard gave a grin and a shrug. "Let's go, Coffin, or we'll be late." The tall, lean man had started calling Lin "Coffin" ever since they'd joined landscaping forces. He opened the passenger door and saw Nicky. "You bringin' this cur with you again?" He gave the dog a gentle push so he could climb in. Nicky sat on Leonard's lap and gave him a lick on the face. Leonard groaned and wiped the spot with his rolled up sleeve. Lin knew that the man secretly liked the friendly creature. She got into the driver's seat, started the engine, and drove down the street heading to their client's home.

Lin and Leonard worked side by side for two hours preparing the soil for the stone blocks. Lin had already learned so much from the experienced landscaper and appreciated that he would share his knowledge with her. She stood and stretched and then walked to the front of the house to get a pry bar from the truck bed. They'd encountered a large rock while digging up the grass and soil and they needed the tool to help loosen the boulder from the ground. Carrying the tool back to the yard, Lin rounded the corner of the house to see Leonard sitting on the grass facing away from her with Nicky perched right next to him pressing his side into the man while Leonard scratched the dog's ears.

Lin's smile faded when she saw the shimmering atoms swirling in the sunlight. The ghost girl appeared thirty feet in front of Leonard and Nicky. The dog wagged his tiny tail and gave a whine.

A cool breeze caused Lin to shiver. She wanted to talk to the girl, but couldn't with Leonard sitting right there. Lin nodded to the ghost and then turned to the man. "I left my heavy bag in the truck. Would you mind grabbing it for me? My lower back is killing me today from all this heavy work."

Leonard gave Lin a suspicious look. "Okay," he said slowly. He walked around the side of the house to the front.

Lin blew out a breath of relief and turned to face the ghost. She gave her a little smile and used a gentle tone of voice. "You're Amanda, right?"

The girl didn't respond.

"I'd like to help." Lin spoke softly. She had to hurry to speak to the ghost because Leonard would be returning any second. "My friend, Leonard, can't see the things that I can see, so I won't be able to talk to you when he comes back. Can you tell me where ..." She wasn't sure how to phrase her question. "Can you tell me where your earthly form is?"

Amanda's eyes peeked out from under her long lashes and she held Lin's gaze, but she didn't speak or gesture.

"Can you take me to the spot where your body is?"

Amanda glanced over Lin's shoulder to the corner of the house. Lin knew that Leonard was coming back. She whispered to the ghost. "Can you come back later? When I'm alone?"

The ghost looked at the little brown dog sitting at Lin's feet.

Lin blinked. "Oh. The dog doesn't count. He's always with me."

"You talkin' to yourself, Coffin?" Leonard placed Lin's heavy bag on the lawn.

"I was singing," Lin fibbed. She walked over to the patio area that they'd been working on.

"Glad I missed that." Leonard lifted the pry bar from the grass and started in on the rock.

Lin thanked him for getting her bag and picked up a tool to help work on loosening the boulder from the ground.

***

LIN MET Viv outside the bookstore and the two walked down the brick sidewalk to the Irish restaurant for drinks, but the real reason was to do some sleuthing. So far, it had been a hot and humid summer but luckily most evenings cooled off and the air was drier and more pleasant. Lin loved the long days and the bustle of the summer with people flocking to the island. Although, many residents didn't care for the tourist season and the huge increase in the population, Lin enjoyed the long summer days, good weather, and the energy of so many people enjoying their time on the island.

When she returned to the island in June, she never considered that she and Viv would be involved in mysteries and murders. She let out a sigh as they opened the door to the restaurant and walked into the room on the right of the entryway that housed the bar section of the space. The girls spotted two people vacating stools at the bar and they hurried over to claim them.

The bar area was done in dark wood and copper details. Modern, high, wooden tables and chairs were grouped around a floor-to-ceiling stone fireplace. The place was packed with people sitting and standing together enjoying drinks and conversation while the Irish music played over the speaker system. Lin was thankful that the music in the place was much less loud than it had been the other night.

The bartender greeted the girls, placed small bowls of nuts and crackers in front of them, and took their orders. The man was in his mid-to-late-forties, but his muscular physique clearly indicated that he was fit and worked out a good deal.

"Maybe we can start by questioning the good-looking bartender." Viv winked. "He might be helpful."

"He looks familiar," Lin noted.

"He's a lifeguard over at Cisco Beach. Every summer, he lifeguards and bartends here on the island and then heads to Florida in the winter to do the same there. Somebody told me that he's been life-guarding on-island for nearly thirty years."

"Well, he's in great shape by the look of it."

There was a lull in orders when the bartender returned with the girl's drinks and he took out a cloth and wiped down the granite counter. Viv started to chat with him and soon the talk went from how business was this summer to a discussion of the news-of-the-day which gave Lin an opening to bring up Amanda.

"You know Amanda Robinson?" Lin ran her finger down the side of her beer glass. "We heard someone reported her missing to the police."

The bartender was holding a glass in one hand and was drying it off with a white cloth. His face clouded for a moment. "She waitresses here. I know who she is, but we don't have much interaction." He nodded across to the lobby. "She was always in the dining room, not in here."

"Have you heard any buzz about her?" Viv took a sip of her wine.

"Nobody says much. Some people think maybe

she had a fight with her boyfriend and just took off. Left the island and went home."

"We heard her boyfriend worked here, too."

"He filled in for a couple of weeks. The group that owns this place owns a few other spots in town. Employees sometimes shuffle around between the restaurants according to need."

"Was Amanda friendly with anyone in particular here?" Viv wondered if there was someone else around who might have more insight.

The guy thought for a minute. "Amanda and Jessie worked a lot of the same shifts. They seemed to get along well."

"Is Jessie working tonight?"

"She's usually on. She's short, has short blonde hair. Looks like a pixie."

Viv chuckled. "How does she manage the heavy trays?"

"You can be short and strong." The bartender smiled and flexed his arm.

"Did Amanda get along with the other employees?" Lin tried to sound nonchalant, like they were only gossiping.

"Seemed to." The guy filled some orders and placed the glasses on the bar for the other customers. "She seemed like a nice girl, no drama, did her work, she seemed pleasant."

"Are people concerned about her disappearance?" Viv questioned. "Or do most think she just took off and didn't tell anyone?"

"It's a mix of opinions. I try not to get involved."

Lin spotted the manager they'd met the other night standing and speaking intently with the hostess and another man at the small counter in the foyer room. "How is it to work here? Good boss?"

The bartender shrugged. "As good as any."

"We were here the other night." Lin rolled her eyes. "The manager wasn't too welcoming."

"He's sort of intense. I do my work, keep out of his way."

Lin looked out to the foyer. "Who's the man the manager is speaking with?" The forty-something man was trim and fit and dressed in a well-fitted suit. He had an air of importance about him.

"That's the president of the Abbott Group. Ken Milliken." The bartender smiled. "I'm just a few years older than him. I knew him from when we started working on-island years ago. We hung out sometimes. The Abbott Group owns a lot of restaurants and clubs here on Nantucket, on Martha's Vineyard, and on the mainland. Ken's a pretty good guy, reasonable, pleasant for the most part, very hands-on. He comes by every week or two to check on things." The bartender chuckled. "Ken did a heck of a lot better than I did. He went up the ranks like a rocket. Made vice-president by the time he was in his mid-twenties." The bartender greeted a regular who took a seat on one of the stools.

Viv eyed the man standing with the manager. "I

think I read an article about him a few years ago. He grew up here on Nantucket, started working for the Abbott Group at one of the restaurants as a bus boy when he was a late teen. He worked his way up through the ranks to president. It was a nice rags-to-riches story."

"Would Ken know anything about Amanda?" Lin asked.

"Nah. He wouldn't know any of the help by name." The bartender glanced out to the entry room. The manager had stepped away from Ken Milliken and was striding into the dining room. "There's Jessie, by the way."

The girls followed his gaze. Lin thought that the bartender's description of the young woman was exactly on target. Jessie did look like a pixie.

"Have the police been here to ask questions about Amanda?" Lin asked.

"Yeah. They asked the same stuff you're asking." The bartender moved down the bar to check on the other customers.

"He's doesn't know much about Amanda," Viv observed.

"Well, he directed us to Jessie. Maybe we'll learn something from her."

Jessie was still at the front desk writing something in a book. Lin raised an eyebrow at her cousin, slid off the stool, and walked into the entry room where she spoke to the blonde girl for a few seconds. The girl looked at Lin with wide eyes, listened, and gave a nod. Lin came back and sat down. “Jessie said she can talk to us after her shift. The restaurant side of the pub closes before the bar.”

Viv groaned. “I have to get up early. Maybe I’ll curl up on that sofa over there and take a nap.”

Lin laughed. “You should have brought a blanket and a pillow.”

The girls chatted for a few more minutes when suddenly Viv’s eyes widened. “Oh, I forgot to tell you. John just got a new listing.” She held her cousin’s eyes and paused for effect.

Lin smiled. “Okay, tell me. I know it must be something interesting.”

“It’s the house behind mine.”

“What?” Lin asked excitedly. “Sebastian and Emily Coffin’s former house?”

The mansion behind Viv’s small Cape house had been built several hundred years ago and during the eighteenth century it had been the home of the girls’ ancestors, Sebastian Coffin and his wife, Emily. An unfortunate bank scandal had caused rumors to spread about Sebastian which resulted in him losing his position at the bank. A reduction in funds necessitated a move from the mansion to the smaller house now owned by Viv.

“What’s the asking price?” Lin lifted her glass to her lips and sipped.

Viv smiled. “Eleven and a half million dollars.”

Lin choked on her swallow of beer and almost

fell off the bar stool.

Viv chuckled at her cousin's reaction and joked, "Want to go in on it with me?"

"Sure." Lin wiped her mouth with a small napkin. "I have five thousand dollars to contribute. Well, probably less than that."

Viv laughed. "I guess we can't buy it then. I was hoping you'd come up with the majority of the funds."

"That family has owned the mansion for ages," Lin observed. "I wonder why they've decided to sell it now."

Viv's eyes twinkled. "John says the owners want out because the house has recently become haunted."

Lin's jaw dropped.

CHAPTER 10

"The house has *recently* become haunted?" Lin's eyes bugged out of their sockets. "How recent?"

The bartender returned and asked if the girls needed another drink. They both declined, referencing their need to rise early for their jobs the next day.

"How recent?" Lin asked a second time.

Viv leaned closer. "Very." She had a serious expression on her face.

"Do you think the ghost in the mansion is Amanda?" Lin's mouth hung open. "What did John say?"

"Not much. We need to talk to him." Viv's phone buzzed with an incoming text. "It's John. He says his friend told him that the missing girl's father has arrived on the island and is demanding that the police find his daughter."

"I would do the same." Lin checked her watch to see how soon Jessie would be getting off her shift. "How does John's friend know what's going on?"

"He works at the police station." Viv smiled.

"John is full of information." She sent her boyfriend a return text. "Let's have dinner together at my house tomorrow night. We can ask John about the mansion and what the owners have told him about it being haunted." She put her phone in her bag. "Is Jeff back from the mainland yet? Bring him, too."

"He won't be back until the day after tomorrow. Why don't you and John come to my house? It's my turn to cook." Lin waved towards the reception desk. "Jessie just gestured to me that she'll be ready in five minutes."

The girls paid their tab and walked outside to the cross street at the corner of the Irish pub where they waited for the young woman to come and meet them. A cool breeze blew off the ocean and Viv pulled her light jacket closed and zipped it. "I hope this meeting is quick. I'm exhausted."

"Here she comes." Lin waved.

Jessie was short and had big brown eyes. Her short hair was nearly platinum blonde and reflected the light of the streetlamp. "Hey." She shoved her hands in the back pockets of her jeans.

Viv and Lin introduced themselves. Lin glanced across the street to the entrance of the pub. "Do you want to go get a coffee? There's the shop just a couple of blocks from here."

The girl shifted from one foot to the other. She seemed hesitant.

"We can't stay long." Lin tried to encourage the

girl. "We have to get up early tomorrow for work."

"Okay. I'm pretty tired. I need to get home, but a quick coffee would be good."

The three of them started down the street. Lin explained how she'd run into Amanda the other night after falling down on the sidewalk. She told Jessie that they'd recently heard that Amanda was missing and realized that she must have disappeared shortly after running into Lin that night. They entered the coffee shop, went to the counter to place their orders, and took their drinks to a small table in the corner.

"I have to say the whole thing really disturbed me." Lin cradled the coffee cup in her hands. "I wonder if I might have been able to help in some way if we hadn't parted when we did."

Jessie sipped from her take-out cup and set it down on the tabletop. "I can't understand what happened." The girl's voice was sweet and it made her seem younger than she was. "I liked Amanda. The shift always went by faster when she was on. She was super friendly and easy to talk to. I thought she must be sick when she didn't come in to work. Then she wasn't there the next day either. I went to the manager and asked about her. He told me she hadn't called in and that he would fire her if she ever showed up again. I thought maybe she got another job. Now I don't know what to think."

"Did you ever hang out with Amanda? Outside of work?" Lin asked.

Jessie shook her head. "I think we would have eventually. We just hadn't got around to it."

"Did she seem herself the last few times you saw her?" Viv questioned.

Jessie looked down at her cup. "Mostly. She seemed a little annoyed with things that last day. She wasn't as happy as usual, but as the shift went on, she was more like herself."

Lin hoped the girl could give more information about Amanda's mood. "Did she say what was bothering her? Did you happen to ask what was up?"

Jessie nodded. "I asked. She kind of blew it off." The young woman's brow furrowed. "Oh, she said something though. It just popped into my head right now. She said something like some people just aren't what they seem. I don't know what she meant. I should have asked her, but the dinner crowd started to come in and we got busy."

"How's your manager to work for?"

Jessie looked surprised and her face hardened. "He's a jerk. You never know what mood he'll be in."

"The other day we met a girl who works in the kitchen." Viv leaned back against her chair. "She said she makes the desserts. She told us that Amanda's boyfriend worked at the pub for a couple of weeks."

"Yeah, he did, but our shifts were different. I didn't get to know him."

"Do you know the girl who makes the desserts?" Lin felt like they weren't getting anywhere.

Jessie shrugged. "I know who you mean. Kathy Lowe. She's not that friendly."

Lin said, "She seemed kind of nervous talking about Amanda's boyfriend. She wouldn't talk to us in front of the pub, like she didn't want anybody to see her with us."

Jessie glanced out the window into the darkness and then turned back to the cousins. "I don't know why that would be."

A chill ran down Lin's spine. She wasn't sure if she could trust this girl or not.

Jessie checked the time on her phone.

Lin asked, "Is there anyone else you can think of that we might talk to about Amanda?"

"Her boyfriend." Jessie shrugged a shoulder. "I don't know who else she hung out with. I need to get going." She got up and started away, but turned back, her face creased with concern. "You don't think anything bad happened to Amanda, do you?"

Lin couldn't keep her eyes from filling up with tears. She blinked a few times.

Viv forced a smile. "She's probably fine."

As she headed for the exit, Jessie gave a slight nod, but she was clearly not convinced.

CHAPTER 11

Lin and Jeff sat with Viv and John around Lin's deck table enjoying their dinner of baked Romano-Parmesan chicken, roasted baby potatoes, green beans almondine, corn on the cob, and fresh baked rolls. Lin had prepared everything after getting home from a long day of gardening. Jeff returned to Nantucket a day earlier than planned and Lin was thrilled to have him back. She smiled across the table at him.

The sun was setting and the sky was a mix of blue, pink, and violet. Lin had set three glass candleholders in the middle of the table and the light of the candles flickered in the gathering dusk.

John took a swallow of the craft beer he'd brought along to share. "So how does it feel to know there are ghosts living in the house behind Viv's yard?" He chuckled. John didn't believe in such things and had no idea that Lin was able to see the spirits of those who had passed.

Viv shot Lin a quick look. "I think it's really interesting."

Jeff didn't know about Lin's skills either. "Some of the antique houses I've worked on here are thought to be haunted."

"I've never run into any ghosts when showing houses to clients." John smiled.

Viv reached for another ear of corn. "What in the world happened to have the family decide to leave the mansion?"

John speared a baby potato with his fork. "Mrs. Abbott insisted on telling me what had been going on recently. She was afraid if they didn't disclose their concerns to the new owner that they'd be opening themselves up for a lawsuit."

Lin's eyes narrowed. "Really? Is that even a possibility?"

John gave a slight shake of his head. "Sellers should disclose things like any problems with the structure or function of a building, if someone had committed suicide on the premises, things like that. But, honestly, ghosts? How many people believe in things like that?"

Lin swallowed hard and the corners of her mouth turned down. John's comment brought up old feelings of childhood rejection that she'd suffered when she shared the fact that she could see spirits. Viv gave her cousin a warning look, afraid she might slip and reveal her abilities to John.

"Lots of people claim to have seen ghosts." Jeff took a swallow of beer.

"What did Mrs. Abbott tell you?" Lin placed her

fork on her plate.

"Strange stuff. Her husband experienced the things as well. She said that their bedroom would suddenly become very cold, almost like their air conditioning had gone haywire. Mrs. Abbott said she woke several times to see a man and a woman in the room, just standing there, watching her and her husband sleep. Mr. Abbott got up to use the bathroom one night and he saw a strange light flickering at the end of the hallway. He went to investigate thinking that they'd left a light on. When he reached the end of the hall, a cool breeze enveloped him and the door to one of the guest bedrooms slammed shut. When he opened the door, the lights and the coldness were gone."

"This had never happened before?" Nicky had come up next to Viv's chair and she scratched his ears.

"Mrs. Abbott said that years ago her mother claimed there had been some paranormal activity in the house when she'd lived there. Mrs. Abbott always brushed it off. When she and her husband moved in, they never experienced anything out of the ordinary. Until recently."

"Is that reason to sell?" Viv questioned. She wondered why the Abbotts were so fearful about some chilly air and flickering lights especially since Mrs. Abbott's own mother had seen and felt similar goings-on when she had resided in the mansion.

"They're spooked." John reached for the serving

platter for another piece of chicken. "This is all delicious, Lin."

Lin thanked him. "Did she bring up anything else? It seems an excessive reaction for them to immediately put their house up for sale. There are lots of stories about haunted houses here on the island. Why do you think the Abbotts are so eager to get away?"

John cleared his throat. "Well, Mr. and Mrs. Abbott lost a daughter. She was twenty-one when she disappeared."

"That's terrible." Lin shook her head. "How long ago did that happen?"

"About twenty-five years ago."

"What's that got to do with flickering lights and two ghosts standing in the couple's bedroom?" Jeff asked.

"Mrs. Abbott told me that some nights she hears the sounds of weeping. It seems like it's coming from the yard. It sounds like a girl, crying as if in terrible distress. Mrs. Abbott only hears it at night and when she looks outside, she doesn't see anyone. It keeps her from sleeping. She said she can't stay in the house with that weeping keeping her up all night."

Lin straightened and her eyes widened. Her heart was beating fast. "Do they think it's their daughter?"

John turned his palms up. "Mrs. Abbott didn't come right out and say as much, but I would think that could be the case."

"What happened to the daughter?" Lin's forehead was lined with concern. "I never heard about this before."

"She just disappeared." John frowned. "She was never found."

"I know about this." Jeff reached across the table to hold Lin's hand. "I was about five or six when it happened. My sister knew the girl. Was her name Madeleine?"

John shrugged.

"Maybe the girl took off?" Viv speculated. "Did she have a boyfriend? Maybe the two of them ran away together."

"I didn't ask for details." John looked like he wished the whole subject would go away. "The Abbotts are staying in a hotel for the rest of the summer and then they're returning to New York. They don't want to be near the mansion anymore. They've hired a firm to remove and sell the furniture after they have an offer on the house."

Lin fidgeted in her seat. "How long has this crying been going on?"

"Not long. A few days."

A chill ran down Lin's back.

"And they've decided to sell because they've heard crying for only a few days?" Viv couldn't believe the couple would rush away over something like that. "What if the noises stop?"

John cocked his head with a sheepish look on his

face. "Well, I sort of hope the noises don't stop. I have a massive commission at stake."

Viv smiled. "That's perfectly understandable, and anyway, you don't have to worry that the Abbotts will change their minds if they aren't staying at the house anymore."

Lin leaned forward with a glint in her eye. "You're probably fine as long as the ghostly crying doesn't start up when you're showing the house to prospective buyers."

John's eyebrows shot up. A horrified look washed over his face.

Viv gave him a playful nudge. "I thought you didn't believe in ghosts?"

John scowled.

Viv put her arm around her boyfriend. "Don't worry. Nothing will mess up your showings." She gave him a peck on his cheek and ruffled his brown hair. "Tell us what your friend heard at the police station about the missing girl."

John took another roll and buttered it. "Rob saw the girl's dad at the station. He heard that Mr. Robinson wants to hire his own private detective to find out where his daughter is. He's very wealthy and he's used to getting his way. He plans to bring the detective over from the mainland. Robinson was ranting at the police chief. He doesn't think the police are doing enough. It was pretty bad, I guess. The media is camping out near the station dying to get their hands on some news."

Nervous energy pulsed through Lin's body. "Does your friend, Rob, know any details? Has he heard anything about what might have happened to Amanda?"

"Listen, don't share anything I tell you." John made eye contact with them. "There's some security video from some of the stores along the route Amanda walked that night. She and her boyfriend walked together for several blocks. Near the end of the tapes that the police have gathered, you can see Amanda moving away from the boyfriend. The guy is standing in the street watching her go. It jives with what the boyfriend claims. He told the police where they split up and it's the same spot in the tapes that shows them going separate ways."

"He could have taken a back street and then caught up with her," Viv said. "They can't discount the boyfriend as a suspect just because he says that's the last he saw of her."

"I'm sure they haven't eliminated him unless he has an alibi." Jeff rubbed his forehead. He looked at Lin. "It's weird that you happened to run into them not long before she went missing."

Lin's face clouded. "I know." She shook herself and looked at John. "Did Rob share anything else?"

"He said the police aren't convinced of foul play. They believe that there's a real possibility she left the island or could even be staying with a friend somewhere here on Nantucket."

"Where would she get her money?" Viv asked. "She's just a college kid."

"Her dad is loaded. Maybe Amanda has a nice fat bank account." John sipped from his glass.

"If she withdrew money then that would alert the police to where she was," Jeff commented. "So it isn't likely that she's accessing a bank account."

"I agree, and honestly?" John made a face. "I think the police need to take this more seriously and treat it as a kidnapping or...." He hesitated. "A murder."

Lin winced.

"You think foul play is involved?" Viv put her hand on John's arm.

"I don't know why, but I feel like nothing good is going to come out of this." John sighed. "I know we're not that much older than Amanda Robinson is, but I feel like she's just a kid. She's in college. We're already working. We have homes of our own. She's just at the very beginning of her life." John shook his head slowly. "Or she was."

Sadness wrapped around Lin's heart.

CHAPTER 12

After finishing the meal and helping to clean up, Jeff headed home to prepare for a new job he was starting on-island tomorrow and John had to leave to go back to his office to finish some paperwork for the next morning. Viv and Lin sat in the kitchen drinking tea. Nicky sat on his dog bed in the corner of the room.

"John thinks Amanda is dead." Viv put her chin in her hand. "It's very hard for me to keep your skills a secret from him."

"Maybe we can tell him one day." Lin pulled her hair back into a ponytail. "If you get engaged, then tell him. I'd rather not share the knowledge of my abilities unless we know the person is going to be part of our family. I wish I could tell Jeff, but it's just too soon."

"I agree." Viv yawned. There had been too many late nights and early mornings recently. "What do you think about the Abbotts and the ghosts and the crying?" Viv shuddered. "That stuff about Mrs. Abbott hearing weeping outside in her yard gave me the willies."

"The ghosts could be Sebastian and Emily Coffin," Lin said. "Anton Wilson's book about haunted places on Nantucket mentioned that the Coffins were thought to haunt the mansion years ago." Lin rubbed her temple. "I really don't like the word "haunt." It has such a negative connotation. There should be a different word to describe a visit from a spirit."

"Hmm," Viv pondered. "How about 'visitation?'"

"There's something odd about that word, too, but it's better than haunt. "Haunt" sounds like the ghost is trying to hurt you."

"I don't think of it that way." Viv looked thoughtful. "The word seems like it means hanging out or showing up on a regular basis. You know, like the phrase "our favorite haunt," meaning a place we hang out."

Lin smiled. "Okay then, I think we should make a visitation to one of our favorite haunts."

Viv cocked her head to the side. "What do you mean?"

"I think it's time to do some investigating."

"Oh, no. It's too late." Viv waved her hand in the air. "We were up so late last night." She leveled her eyes at her cousin. "What do you have in mind?"

Lin grinned. "Hanging out in your backyard. I want to hear the crying that Mrs. Abbott claims to hear. Your backyard abuts their property so we should be able to hear if anyone is weeping." Lin's face turned serious. "I want to know if it's Amanda."

"Do you think it's her?" Viv looked wary.

"It seems like a good chance it's her. Mrs. Abbott said it has only been going on for a few days. The timing is interesting." Lin slid off the counter stool. "You can go to bed, if you want. I'll just pull a chair up to the fence at the back of your yard and sit there for a while."

"How long is a while?" Viv rinsed her mug in the sink.

"Not sure." Lin picked up her sweater and house keys. "Nicky, want to come?"

The little brown dog jumped to his feet and wagged his tiny tail.

Viv breathed a heavy sigh and followed Lin and the dog into the living room and out the front door. "Why does everything have to be done at night?"

***

THE NIGHT air still carried the warmth and humidity of the day as Lin carried one of Viv's deck chairs to the back of her yard and placed it next to the fence. "Have you ever looked over the fence?"

"No. I didn't think the Abbotts would appreciate a Peeping Tom." Viv, Nicky, and Queenie watched Lin as she climbed up on the chair trying to peek into the next yard.

"Have you met the Abbotts?" Lin stretched her neck.

Viv smirked. "Only in passing. Once, at an event at the Historical Museum and another time at a thing at the Whaling Museum. We were introduced and shook hands, said a few pleasantries. I'm not exactly in their social circle."

"There are so many trees on the property line." Lin tried to shimmy up the fence, but slid back and fell on her butt.

Viv chuckled. "There's probably a reason for the trees."

Lin looked up at her cousin from her seat on the lawn. "What would that reason be?"

Viv smiled and cocked her head. "Maybe, and this is just a guess, to keep people from spying into their yard?"

Lin stood and dusted off her butt. "I don't suppose I could go around to the other street and slip into the backyard from the front of the mansion."

"Not unless you want to get arrested for trespassing." Viv had her arms wrapped around herself. "Why is it still so warm out? It's very uncomfortable."

Lin had her ear pressed against the tall white fence. "Shh." She held her index finger to her lips. After a few moments, Lin waved Viv over. She whispered. "Listen. Can you hear anything?"

Viv pressed her ear to the space between the

fence slats. "It's just the breeze."

"Is it?" Lin lifted the chair and headed back to return it to the deck. "I'm going over there."

"Oh, no," Viv moaned. She followed after her cousin. "I'm not going with you."

Lin eyed her. "The Abbotts moved out. They're in a hotel. Who would spot us?"

Viv waved her hand around in the air. "People walking by on the sidewalk, the neighbors, a police patrolman. I don't want to end up arrested. I own a business."

"We'll be stealthy." Lin put the chair down on the deck next to the patio table. "Anyway, if you got arrested, it might be good for business. People would come into the bookstore to get a look at the law breaker."

"Not funny." Viv's face was serious and her arms were tight around her in a defensive posture.

"Will you walk around the block to the front of the mansion with me?" Lin asked.

"You're trying to trick me into sneaking into the Abbotts' yard."

"No, I...." Lin's face brightened. "The ladder. In the storage room." She jogged over to the ell that was built off the back of Viv's house and opened the door. She flicked the light on and moved boxes and furniture pieces aside to reach the ladder. She lifted it and stepped outside.

Viv stood in front of her. "You're using the ladder to go over the fence?" She touched the side of her face and sighed. “What if you get caught? You won’t be able to climb back over the fence. You’ll be stuck there in the yard.” Viv pressed her lips together in a worried expression.

“It’ll be okay.” Lin touched her cousin’s arm reassuringly. “Will you steady the base of the ladder for me?”

Viv walked slowly behind Lin to the rear of the yard. Lin propped the ladder against the fence. “If you could just hold it here.”

Viv stepped over and as Lin moved up the rungs, she put her hands on the sides to keep it from slipping on the fence. “Be careful. Don’t break your leg when you jump down on the other side.”

Nicky watched his owner reach the top of the ladder and he let out a whine. Queenie ran to a nearby tree and climbed up and out on a long limb that grew over the fence. Viv saw the cat high in the tree. “I wish I could do that,” she muttered. “Keep an eye on her, Queenie.”

Lin hung on to the top of the fence and awkwardly positioned herself to leap over. She took a deep breath and jumped, hitting the ground with a thud that knocked the wind out of her. She lost her balance and fell on her side.

Viv whispered through the slats. “Are you in one piece?”

“Barely.” Lin rubbed her ankle and gently put weight on it.

“Stay that way. I’m going to sit here until you

come back."

Lin hobbled off through the trees. Her ankle felt better as she moved along. She pushed some branches aside and entered the backyard of the huge house. It was much bigger than she expected and the grounds had an extensive lawn, a water feature, and landscaped garden beds running around the edges of the space. Flowers were in abundance and blooming hydrangea bushes stood along one side of the yard. In the darkness, Lin hugged the edge of the property as she made her way to the back of the mansion. Every few yards, trying to stay in the shadows, she stopped to listen.

She approached a large stone patio with expensive looking outdoor furniture that had been placed in small groupings. Lin turned her attention to the enormous house with the widow's walk built around the chimney. Taking a few steps closer, Lin froze. She could hear a young woman weeping and the sound of it made the tiny hairs on her arms stand up.

Lin took slow steps in the direction of the crying, but when she reached the far corner of the mansion, the sound seemed to emanate from Lin's original position. She returned to the corner where she had started and then the weeping seemed to come from the side of the home where Lin had just been.

A cool whoosh of air blew past her. Lin glanced around trying to see if a spirit may have come close and she saw the flash of a young woman dash around the side of the mansion. Her dark brown hair flowed down her back as she ran. Lin moved quickly to the other side of the house, but once there, no one was in sight. Her heart pounded with unease and frustration.

An oddly cold breeze washed over Lin's skin and she turned around slowly to see Amanda standing on the patio staring at her with big, round eyes. The corners of Lin's mouth curved up. "Amanda," Lin whispered. She took a step toward the ghost girl, but Amanda shook her head and then her form started to shimmer and become more see-through.

"Stay," Lin urged. Her heart sank when the ghost disappeared into the night. Letting out a long, low sigh, Lin started for the front of the house, but halted when she became enveloped in a pocket of icy air. She whirled around hoping to see that Amanda had returned, but what she saw caused her jaw to drop and her heart beat to speed up. On the spot where Amanda had appeared, stood Sebastian Coffin.

The eighteenth-century ghost was dressed in black trousers and a morning coat and he made eye contact with Lin, gave her a little smile, and made an ever so slight bow before the atoms of his image sparkled and spun and rose into the air where they disappeared.

Lin's breath caught in her throat and then slowly a wide grin spread over her face.

Sebastian.

A gruff male voice spoke behind Lin and caused her to jump. She wheeled around to see a tall, medium built man in his late sixties or early seventies standing before her in the shadows. He had on well-cut dark trousers and a fitted, crisp white button-down shirt. "What are you doing back here?" he growled causing Lin to take a step back.

Her heart was pounding and she stammered, "I ...I...." Lin set her shoulders and drew herself up in order to appear less timid. "Who are you?"

"I should be asking *you* that question since you're on my property." The man scowled and pulled his phone from his pocket.

Lin was about to speak when a dog's bark rang through the air and Nicky pushed his head out from a bush close to where Lin and the older man were standing. The dog made eye contact with his owner and Lin understood.

"There you are." Lin walked to the bush and scooped the little brown dog from his hiding place under the greenery. She turned to the man with a story to cover her reason for being on the premises. "We were walking and he slipped out of his collar. He ran into your yard. I'm very sorry. I should have rung the bell and asked permission before coming back here, but the house looked dark and I didn't think anyone was at home." Carrying the dog, Lin hurried for the front of the mansion. "I'll be sure to get a better-fitting collar," she called over her shoulder. "Sorry, again."

Abbott stared at Lin as she scurried away.

When they reached the sidewalk in front of the massive home, she placed the dog on the walkway and blew out a breath. "Whew. Thanks, Nick." She winked at the creature. "Abbott fell for it." As the two headed up the dark street and around the block, the leaves on the overhanging branches rustled and whispered in the chilly late-night breeze.

When Lin and Nicky arrived back at Viv's yard, they found Viv snoring in the chair by the fence. A bit of drool coated the corner of her open mouth. Lin smiled and gently touched her cousin's shoulder. "Good thing I didn't need help or anything."

Viv started. Disoriented, she blinked a few times and then pushed herself up in the chair. "Are you okay?" Viv flicked her long bangs away from her forehead. "I fell asleep."

"We noticed." Lin and the dog exchanged looks.

Queenie jumped down from the tree near the fence. Lin nodded at the gray cat. She knew the feline had been monitoring her investigation of the Abbott's property and probably alerted Nicky to her plight of being found by Mr. Abbott.

"What happened?" Viv stood up and rubbed at her eyes.

Lin eased the ladder onto the grass, picked up the chair, and carried it back to the deck. She reported what she'd seen in the garden of the mansion and how Nicky showed up to provide a reason for Lin being in the Abbott's backyard.

"Good dog." Viv opened the back door and dragged herself into the house. She couldn't keep a yawn from escaping. "Another ghost? Ugh. What's going on?"

"I think it must be the ghost of the Abbott's daughter."

Viv climbed up the staircase to the second floor bedrooms with Lin and Nicky and Queenie following behind. Viv gestured to the guest room on the right of the landing. "There are fresh linens on the bed. If you want some pajamas, there are some in the dresser." She looked at her cousin. "Why has the daughter shown up now, after all these years?"

"That's a very good question." Lin shrugged.

"I'm going to collapse from exhaustion." Viv headed for her bedroom door, but before entering she turned back with a smile. "I'm glad you saw Sebastian."

Lin returned the smile. "Me, too."

CHAPTER 13

The next evening, Lin sat at a café table with Libby Hartnett and Anton Wilson explaining to them what she'd learned so far. Libby and Anton sat listening with serious expressions. "We're no closer to finding out who killed Amanda, but at least I saw Sebastian."

"It's odd that he has returned to the Abbott's mansion." Anton's eyed flicked about behind the lenses of his glasses. "Sebastian and his wife, Emily, had been seen in the house for years and then they were gone. It must be about forty years since they've been seen in the Abbott place. Odd." He lifted his slender arm and his hand adjusted the frame of his glasses. "Odd, I must say."

"There are plenty of questions and not enough answers." Libby's blue eyes blazed. She glanced at Anton. "We need to take a drive. With Carolin."

"It's too late now," Anton said. "She'll be getting ready to retire soon."

"What?" Lin looked from Libby to Anton. "Drive where? Who is *she*?"

Libby looked kindly at Lin. "There's someone we want you to meet, a friend of ours."

Lin's eyes widened. "Is this the person who can see ghosts?"

Libby nodded. "She's very old and quite frail. It isn't often that she is up for visitors, but I think we need to call on her. Perhaps, tomorrow. I'll see to it."

"The sooner the better, really." Anton lifted the tea cup to his lips. "We need to narrow down some suspects." He opened his leather folder and removed a sheet of white paper and a silver pen. "I'm putting the boyfriend at the top." He wrote on the paper.

"His name is Brian," Lin told Anton. "Brian Murphy."

"Who else?" Anton tapped the pen against the paper.

Lin leaned forward. "I get negative vibes from the manager at the Irish pub where Amanda worked. He seems like a creep. He wasn't helpful at all when we went there to ask about Amanda."

Anton wrote "manager" on the list. "Keep going. Just let your mind free-think. Don't dismiss anything."

"What about Jessie?" Viv came up to the table from having been in her office where she'd been doing paperwork. "She claims to have been Amanda's friend, but who knows? There was something about her that I didn't like." Viv sat down in the chair between Libby and Anton. "I think she's leaving things out."

"And that girl from the pub who didn't want anyone to see her talking to us." Lin's face clouded. "She seemed nervous. What could be the reason for that?"

"Do you know where Amanda lived?" Libby asked. "Maybe you should go talk to her housemates."

"Good idea," Viv said. "I think we should talk to the boyfriend again, too. He might know more than he's saying."

Lin had a faraway look on her face. "What about the new ghost?" She turned to Anton. "Do you know anything about the Abbott's missing daughter? Do you remember the case? Did they ever find a body? Did they think she ran away?"

Anton fidgeted. "Not much was ever determined in that case." His lips were two tight lines on his face.

Lin sensed tension in Anton's body language. "What's wrong?"

"Nothing." Anton's voice sounded an octave higher and had an almost urgent tone like he was too eager to dismiss the question. He sat ramrod straight and started shuffling his papers.

Lin made eye contact with Libby who gave a tiny shrug. Libby put her hand on Anton's arm. "It's not your fault, Anton."

Anton's face flushed red and his wiry frame

seemed to surge with anxiety. To Lin, what he was giving off was almost palpable. Anton got up from his chair so abruptly that it almost toppled. "I'm going to the restroom."

Lin watched him rush away with her mouth hanging open. She looked at Libby for an explanation, but the older woman just shook her head. "He'll tell you someday." Libby pushed a lock of her white-gray hair behind her ear. She turned her eyes on Lin. "You need to be careful with this case." She glanced at Viv. "You, too. There are dangerous forces at work here. I feel that it runs deep. Be careful who you trust. Keep your guard up." Libby swallowed the last of her tea just as Anton returned. He stood next to the table collecting his papers and leather folder.

"I need to get going." Anton nodded at the women around the table and dashed out of the bookstore.

"I need to be going as well." Libby stood. "I'll let you know if we're going to take a drive to visit our friend tomorrow."

When Libby disappeared around the bookshelves, Lin sighed. "That was a weird meeting with those two."

"What's up with Anton?" Viv looked over her shoulder to be sure no one was around. "Does he feel somehow responsible for the Abbott's missing daughter? That's what it seemed like. What in the world could have happened?"

A shudder washed over Lin and she placed her palms on the tabletop to steady herself. "Viv, could all of these things be related?"

Viv's forehead creased in confusion. "What things are related? How? What do you mean?"

Nicky sat up on the easy chair and let out an uncharacteristic howl that caused Lin and Viv to whirl around. Queenie leaped up on the back of the chair and hissed. Lin stood, goose bumps forming on her arms.

Viv reached for her cousin's hand and whispered, "What's going on? What's wrong with the animals?"

Viv's boyfriend appeared at the end of the aisle of bookshelves and, spotting the girls, he hurried to their café table, a strange, pinched look on his face.

Viv's breath caught in her throat and her eyes went wide. Lin stared at him and waited.

John was breathing hard. His pale face was a sharp contrast against the dark brown of his hair. He kept his voice low. "There's a body."

Viv slowly rose from her seat. "They found Amanda?"

John shook his head. "No."

"Who is it then?" Viv questioned.

A heavy weight seemed to be crushing Lin's chest and she couldn't get any words to leave her throat. It felt like an eternity before John finally spoke. "It's the boyfriend. He's dead."

Viv gasped. Her hand flew to her mouth and she

sank into her chair.

Lin's vision was all watery and she blinked hard to clear her sight. "Brian's dead? How? Did he commit...?"

John knew what Lin was about to ask. He cut her off and shook his head. "No. We found him just a while ago. In the house I was showing."

"What?" Lin sucked in a breath. "*You* found him?" She felt awful for John to have come upon the body of Brian Murphy.

John sank into the chair that Anton had vacated. He put his elbow on the table and rested his chin in his hand. "I feel sort of sick."

Viv hurried to the café counter and retrieved a glass of water for her boyfriend. She set it on the table in front of him and then wrapped her arms around his shoulders.

John sipped the water. "Sorry. I got kind of dizzy for a second." His hand was shaking when he placed the glass down.

"Where were you?" Viv's big eyes were full of concern. "Were you alone?"

John shook his head. "I had clients with me. We met Shirley Calder at the house. She's the listing agent. The house has been empty for a while." John's throat seemed to constrict and he coughed hard and took a gulp of water. "We went inside. Shirley was giving her spiel about the house. She opened the door to the half bath on the first floor." John stopped talking and his whole body shuddered. "I'll never forget the sound of her scream."

Viv gripped John's arm and rubbed it. The three sat in silence for a few moments.

"The kid was in the bathroom. He'd been stabbed in the throat." John winced recalling the sight of the dead body.

"Oh, John. I'm so sorry you had to see that." Viv's eyes brimmed with tears.

Lin had a million questions, but she didn't feel she could interrogate John in his shocked state so she sat quietly.

"Where was the house?" Viv's lower lip trembled. "Who owns it?"

John took in a long, slow breath. "It's an antique Cape over on Tangerine Street. The woman who owns it has moved to the mainland to live with her daughter. It's been empty for about a month." Perspiration beaded on John's forehead.

"You called the police?" Viv still held John's arm.

"Yeah. Shirley was still screaming and the man I was showing the house to needed to sit down on the floor while his wife tended to him. It was a mess. I made the call. It seemed like forever for the police to show up, but I know in reality it was barely ten minutes."

"They questioned all of you?" Lin asked.

John gave a nod. "They took statements and then said we could go, but they might want to speak to us again." He managed a smile. "I guess I won't be seeing those clients again any time soon."

"Did you overhear anything the police said?" Lin wondered if the police had anyone in mind as a suspect and might have discussed it within earshot of John.

"I really didn't hear anything. It felt like my head was full of cotton. It still does. Sorry."

"Amanda and Brian both murdered." Viv passed her hands over her eyes. "How can it be?"

"We don't know for sure that Amanda was murdered," John said. "She still might turn up."

Viv went pale realizing that she'd forgotten for a second that John didn't know about Amanda's ghost.

"I think we know that the chances of Amanda being found alive are slim to none." Lin leaned forward. "But *why* is the real question. Why both of them? Obviously, someone needed them dead, but why? Did they stumble upon something? Were they up to something that somebody didn't like?"

Viv and John looked dumbfounded. John asked, "What could they have stumbled on that was so serious that they got killed over it?"

"That's what I need to figure out." Lin stood up. "I'm going over to Tangerine Street."

"Not me." John slowly shook his head. "I'm never going over there again."

"Can it wait?" Viv looked at her cousin.

"I don't think it can. Is it okay if Nicky stays with you?"

"Of course." Viv nodded.

As she turned for the exit, Lin put her hand on Viv's shoulder and said softly, "Take care of John."

CHAPTER 14

Lin practically jogged through town heading for Tangerine Street. A cool breeze off the ocean sent shivers over her skin. When she turned the corner, she could see that a crowd of people had gathered under a streetlight on the opposite side of the road from the house where the young man had been found murdered. She slowed her pace so that she could try to pick up on what people were saying as they passed by her on the dark sidewalk.

Lin took up a spot on the sidewalk at the edge of the crowd. She glanced at the house. It seemed that every light was on inside illuminating the interior so that Lin could see the shadows of police officers and other authority figures passing by the windows. Imagining the scene inside the home caused her to shudder. She sucked in a deep breath, turned, and scanned the people who were standing in small groups chatting and whispering with each other.

She spotted a familiar form leaning against the rough bark of a tall, thick tree. Lin walked up to him. "Hey."

Leonard turned to her. "Hey back at you."

"Gawking?" Lin asked.

"Yup. You, too?"

"Yes. What have you heard?" Lin kept gazing around at the people trying to see if anyone she recognized had joined the crowd.

"Not much." Leonard's eyes narrowed. "You know who they found in there?"

Lin nodded. "Now two young people are dead."

"Don't be so negative, Coffin. They haven't found the girl's body. She might be alive."

Lin held Leonard's eyes and she cocked her head.

The tall man scowled. "It's possible." He shrugged. "Well, isn't it?"

"No." Lin scanned the groups of people again. "I wish it was possible, but it's not." She looked at Leonard. "Why are you in town?"

"I drive in sometimes." Leonard's jaw gave a twitch. "I had a beer down at the docks. It's somethin' to do. Gets me out of the house."

Lin studied the man's face for a minute. Leonard had a sadness that sometimes came over him when he didn't think anyone was paying attention. "Do you have any family on-island?"

"Nah. I moved here with my wife. She was a native, convinced me to live here."

"Where'd you come from?"

"Western Massachusetts. All my family is gone

now."

"Mine, too. Except for Viv." Lin pushed her hair back from her face. "You know Libby Hartnett from town? She told me that she and I are distant relatives. Very distant."

Leonard stared at Lin. "Ms. Hartnett? And you?"

Lin eyed him. "Yeah, why?"

Leonard shifted his attention back to the house. "Interestin.' That's all."

"You've lived on-island for a long time?" Lin asked.

"For forty years."

Lin's jaw dropped. "How old were you when you got married? Five?"

Leonard let out a guffaw and quickly stifled himself when some people on the edge of the gawkers turned and gave him a disapproving look. "I was twenty."

"You're sixty? I don't believe it."

"You gotta believe it." Leonard pushed off the tree and stood straight. "Ain't got my birth certificate on me at the moment."

Lin smiled and then shifted topic. "You know the island, the people here. What in the world is going on? Why would someone want these two kids dead?"

Leonard flicked his eyes at the young woman standing next to him. "I haven't been able to figure evil out yet."

A hearse was parked at the curb at the front of the house and a flurry of activity near the door of the home caused a murmur to run through the crowd and the members of the media to push forward. A police officer stretched out his arms and herded them back while cameras flashed and the momentary brightness lit up the sidewalk near the hearse. Several men carried a stretcher through the doorway and down the stairs to the walkway that led to the curb. A form was visible on the stretcher and was covered by a white sheet tightly tucked under the body. Some people gasped.

"Another young life cut short." Leonard sighed.

Lin turned to look at him and noticed the sag in his shoulders. His posture and the sorrowful tone of his voice caused Lin's heart to squeeze.

"I'm headin' home." Leonard started away from the crime scene. As he walked away, he said over his shoulder, "Don't stay up all night, Coffin. Otherwise you'll be good for nuthin' tomorrow."

Lin smiled. "Good night, Leonard." For a minute, she watched him walk away and then decided to move closer to the groups of people standing further down the street so that she could listen to what was being said. Lin moved her eyes over the crowd. Someone caught her attention and she flicked her gaze back to a lone woman positioned away from the others. Lin squinted and recognized the person as the young woman who made the desserts at the Irish pub and who had spoken to her and Viv late the other night a few blocks from the restaurant. *Kathy Lowe.*

Kathy had a dour look on her face and she jumped when Lin approached and said her name.

The girl's eyes narrowed and then her puzzlement cleared. "Oh," was all she said.

Lin took a step closer. "You heard it was Brian Murphy?"

"Yeah. I just got off work." Kathy turned her gaze back to the house across the street. "I heard people talking as I walked home. I took a detour over here to see if it was true." The young woman had on a well-worn, dark brown sweater and her hands were shoved deep into the pockets.

"Had you seen Brian recently?" Lin kept her eyes on Kathy.

"No."

"It's pretty strange that somebody wanted Brian *and* Amanda out of the picture."

Kathy looked at Lin. "They found Amanda?"

"No. But if Brian's been killed, well, I…."

"You can't assume the same thing happened to Amanda." Kathy's eyes darkened. "She might have just taken off, gone back home."

"Amanda's father arrived on the island the other day demanding that the police find his daughter, so she obviously didn't go home."

Kathy let out a noise that seemed a cross between a groan and a hiss. She seemed as sullen as she had the previous time Lin had spoken with her, but there was something more that the young woman was giving off, an edginess or sparks of nervousness that Lin couldn't quite figure out. It was something other than a sense of shock or upset over the killing. Standing next to Kathy made Lin uncomfortable and she had to force herself to stay and not move away.

The muscles in Kathy's cheek twitched.

"Do you have any ideas about what might have been going on with Amanda and Brian?"

Kathy flashed Lin a look. "How would I know?"

"You worked with them. Did you ever pick up on any odd behavior or hear parts of conversations that might suggest a motive?" Instinct told Lin to step back, but she held her ground.

"Are you a detective or something? Or maybe you just like playing detective?" Kathy's expression was so hard and cold that a chill ran down Lin's back.

"You don't have to be snippy. Won't it help the police if we think things over and try to help with this? Any little thing can sometimes break a case open and lead to the killer." Lin crossed her arms over her chest. "Isn't it everyone's responsibility to look out for others?" Anger bubbled up in Lin's throat. "If it was my sibling or my friend, or ... me, I'd want people to do what they could to help."

Kathy seemed to soften for a second and her mouth opened, but she changed her mind and closed it. She pinched the bridge of her nose. "I need to go home. I've had enough. I'm getting a headache."

Lin wasn't sure if Kathy meant she'd had enough of the events of the past few days or she'd had enough of talking to Lin. As Kathy moved away, Lin asked, "Are you okay?"

Kathy looked back. "No, I'm not. And if you're smart, you'll watch what you're stepping into." She hurried away taking furtive glances at the crowd as she went.

Confusion washed over Lin and her throat tightened. *Is she threatening me?*

CHAPTER 15

Wondering if she was at the right house, Lin glanced at the directions on the paper on the passenger seat as she pulled her truck over and parked at the curb just as Libby Hartnett and Anton Wilson came to a stop behind her. It had taken about twenty minutes to drive to Siasconset, called 'Sconset, which was located at the eastern end of Nantucket. The village had been settled as a fishing area in the seventeenth century and a whaling station was located there during the eighteen-hundreds. The village's name came from the Native American Wampanoag Algonquin tribe's words meaning "place of great bones."

Many of the silver-gray shingled cottages and bungalows in 'Sconset had pink-red roses growing up and over the roofs of the small houses. Some of the rose bushes were so large and had so many roses growing on them that Lin was often sure that the roofs would collapse from bearing the weight of the blooming bushes. Only on Nantucket had Lin ever seen rose bushes climbing up the sides of houses, sprawling up one part of the roof and over and down onto the other slope. Lin thought that the roses were one of the many aspects of the little village that made the place magical.

Lin had spent the morning with Leonard working on resetting the stones of a client's patio and the afternoon was filled with deadheading blooms, watering flowers, and mowing lawns at the homes of several of her customers. She had just enough time to run home for a quick shower and snack before she made the drive to the other end of the island to meet Libby and Anton for the visit with their friend. Lin couldn't shake off the butterflies of nervousness dancing in her stomach. She'd never met anyone who could see ghosts as she did. She slid out from the driver's seat and greeted the two people as they headed over to her truck.

Libby was dressed in loose linen slacks and a pale blush-colored blouse. Without even saying hello she started in on what Lin should and should not do during the meeting, which did not help Lin's nerves in the least. Libby took Lin's elbow and steered her to the front door of the rose-covered cottage with Anton following behind.

Libby chattered away. "Don't touch her unless she reaches out for you. Don't ask her questions. Don't pity her. Don't stare at her."

Lin's eyes went wide and her heart thudded like a booming drum.

"Honestly, Libby," Anton said. "You're going to frighten Carolin away."

Libby waved her hand to dismiss the man's comment. "Carolin isn't so easily frightened. She isn't made of sugar, you know."

Lin muttered, "Maybe I am."

Libby rang the bell and the door was opened by a petite white-haired woman with a wide, welcoming smile. Thinking this was the woman they'd come to visit, Lin exhaled audibly, relieved by the sight of the friendly person.

Libby introduced the two. "Lin, this is Agnes, Liliana's housekeeper and attendant."

Lin's heart sank on hearing that this wasn't Liliana. She shook hands.

"Lovely to meet you, dear." Agnes stepped back to allow the guests to enter. "Lily is outside on the patio." She led them through a cozy living room to the back of the house. Huge windows provided a beautiful view out over the ocean. Lin spotted a frail woman sitting in a wheelchair on the patio. Her knees were covered by a plaid blanket and she had a cream-colored shawl draped over her shoulders. The old woman's white head was hanging to the side at an awkward angle. The four people stepped outside from the house and Agnes walked softly to the wheelchair, bent, and gently touched the cheek of the sleeping woman.

Liliana stirred.

"Libby and Anton are here."

"Hmm?"

"You have visitors. Libby and Anton."

Liliana didn't respond.

"And a friend," Agnes said.

Liliana's eyes popped open. She sat straighter in the chair, blinked and looked around.

"Here she is." Agnes gestured to Lin.

Liliana made eye contact with the young woman and Lin felt like she was standing alone in the center of a bright light, with glimmering warmth spreading through her body. She tried to open her mouth to speak, but her lips only trembled.

"Sit here, dear." Agnes pulled a lawn chair over and placed it beside the wheelchair.

Lin moved to the chair and sat down. She waited for Liliana to speak to her, but the old woman just stared out at the ocean and after a few minutes, Lin shifted her gaze to the sea and the two sat in silence. Lin couldn't remember ever feeling so peaceful.

Libby, Anton, and Agnes sat quietly at the patio table. No one was sure how much time had passed when Liliana shifted slightly in her seat.

Keeping her eyes looking out at the sea, the frail woman said in a voice so soft that she could barely be heard. "There are people who can help you. But, be careful, Carolin. There are many that you cannot trust." Liliana seemed to run out of breath and she paused for several minutes. "Some of us can see what others cannot. Your gift will become stronger." A smile spread over the old woman's face. "Soon I will pass to the other side and you will take my place. I'm very glad that you are here." She lifted a shaky arm from her lap and reached her hand out. "Take my hand."

Lin shifted around in her seat and leaned forward. She held out her hand and let the woman's bony hand rest against her palm. As soon as their skin touched, Lin's vision dimmed and all she could see were swirling lights that seemed to explode inside her brain and fill her head with colors. In a moment, the colors faded and Lin's vision returned to normal.

Liliana slumped in her chair. Agnes tipped a glass of water to the woman's lips. Lin shook off the odd feeling of having been asleep for hours. She turned to look at Libby and Anton.

Libby rose from her seat and walked over to Lin. "Carolin, would you wait out front for us?"

Lin didn't understand why she had to leave, but she did what she was asked. She glanced at Liliana, wanting to thank her for the visit, but the woman's eyes were still closed. Agnes gave Lin a warm smile and a nod, so Lin walked slowly back into the house, went through the living room, and out the front door. She was about to sit down on the stoop when movement near the flower beds at the side of the house caught her eye. Leonard knelt beside the bed pulling out dead blooms and replacing them with fresh flowers.

Lin walked over. “Leonard?”

Leonard looked up with a start. “I didn’t hear you, Coffin. You have a sneaky step.” He stood and wiped his soil-covered palms on his jeans. “I saw your truck. Figured you were here for a visit.”

“You work here?” Her surprise at seeing Leonard was evident on her face.

“I’ve been doing her gardening for years.”

“Why didn’t you tell me?”

Leonard’s eyebrows went up and he gave a shrug. “I don’t know who all your clients are. It’s not very interestin’ information. Why would you want to know?”

Lin’s mouth opened and then shut. Leonard was right. Why would they tell each other who all their clients were?

“I’m just surprised to see you.” Lin rubbed her forehead.

“You okay?”

“Yeah.” Lin smiled. “Just a bit of a headache.”

“You have a nice visit?” Leonard eyed Lin.

“Yeah. It was short though.”

“Liliana’s a nice lady. She’s helped me a lot.” Leonard shook his head. “She’s doing poorly. She isn’t long for this world.” He looked at the waves crashing against the rocks below Liliana’s property. A seagull cried out overhead. “Things change.”

They heard the slap of the screen door and Libby and Anton came down the front steps. The rims of Libby’s eyes were red. She hurried to the passenger side of Anton's car, opened the door, and got in.

Anton nodded towards Lin. "We're heading home. We'll be in touch." He got into his vehicle and they drove away.

Leonard watched the car turn the corner. "Change can be hard." He gave Lin a wistful look and a corner of his mouth turned up. "But we carry each other along."

Lin cocked her head. "Have you become a philosopher when I wasn't looking?"

Leonard knelt down beside the flower bed and picked up his trowel. "Can't just work in the dirt all the time, you know."

Lin watched the man dig in the soil, her mind working, something picking at her.

Leonard glanced up at her. "Something wrong, Coffin?"

"You got stabbed last month, when you came to warn me about Greg Hammond's killer."

"Got the scar to prove it, too."

Lin narrowed her eyes. "How'd you heal so fast?"

Leonard sat back on his heels. "I have a healthy constitution." He reached out and deadheaded several blooms. "There was a lot of blood, but the knife wound wasn't deep." He chuckled. "No magic involved, if that's what you're worried about."

Lin could feel things swirling in the air. She couldn't grasp at the flickers and she knew she was missing something. Her face scrunched up as she pondered what was picking at the back of her brain.

Without looking up, Leonard said, "You just gonna' stand there and supervise me for the rest of the evening?"

"Huh?" Lin shook herself. "Oh. No, I'm going home now. See you tomorrow."

Out of the corner of his eye, Leonard watched Lin head to her truck, get in, turn down the street, and disappear.

He turned back to his work and smiled.

CHAPTER 16

"The knife wound wasn't as bad as it seemed, that's all." Viv passed the bowl of rice to her cousin. "Why are you making such a big deal about it?"

Lin spooned a hearty portion of rice onto her plate. "Leonard works hard. He doesn't sit at a desk all day. How did he heal fast enough to get back to work so quickly?"

"Just like he said. He's healthy, the wound wasn't deep." Viv shrugged and then narrowed her eyes. "What's the big deal? What are you getting at?"

Lin used tongs to remove a chicken breast from the serving platter and she placed it on her plate. "I feel like I'm missing something important."

"Well, you might be." Viv cut a small piece of chicken and raised her fork to her mouth. "But it probably doesn't involve Leonard."

Lin chewed and pondered. "What about Kathy Lowe? What do you think about the conversation I had with her?"

"I think she's weird and guilty." Viv sipped from

her glass of lemon water.

"What's the motive?" Lin asked.

Viv pursed her lips. "She fell in love with Brian and needed to get Amanda out of the way."

Lin stared at Viv. "I don't think Brian was Kathy's type."

Viv tilted her head. "Okay. Kathy fell in love with *Amanda*. Amanda didn't reciprocate. Kathy flew into a rage and killed Amanda. Brian found out so Kathy had to kill him, too."

Lin's eyes went wide. "Yikes. Could that have happened?"

"Kathy seems hard and cold. Given the right circumstances, I can see her as a killer." Viv reached for another serving of grilled asparagus.

"I don't know. We need to find out more," Lin said. Nicky sat down next to the patio table in case a piece of chicken fell to the floor. Lin scratched his ears. "I'd also like to learn more about the new ghost at the Abbott's house. And why Anton acted so weird about her. Let's search the internet after dinner. There must be some information online about the Abbott's daughter and her disappearance."

"You asked me earlier if I thought there could be connections between things." Viv placed her fork on her plate. "I've been thinking about it and I wonder. The Abbotts have recently heard crying in their backyard and a new ghost has appeared there. Is there a connection between what's going on at the Abbott's mansion and what happened to Amanda and Brian?"

"I've been wondering the same thing." Lin rubbed her temple. "This mess might be more complicated than we thought." She clutched her hands together in her lap, worry etched over her face. Her lower lip started to tremble.

Viv stared at her cousin. "What's the matter with you?"

Lin blinked. "Liliana said I would take her place. I don't know what she means. What if I can't do what's necessary ... or expected? Whatever that may be."

Viv held Lin's eyes. "You'll be able to. Liliana wouldn't have said it if she didn't think it would be so. You'll figure it out. It will probably take time, maybe a very long time, but you'll be able to do what you're supposed to do. What you need to do." Viv nodded. "I know it."

Lin's throat tightened with emotion and it was hard to get the words out. "You're good to me." She knew it was an inadequate expression of what she felt, but it was all she was able to manage.

Viv smiled. "Let's figure out this case."

The girls finished their meals and cleaned up. Once the leftovers were put away and everything was in the dishwasher, they opened Viv's laptop and sat next to each other at the kitchen table as Lin's fingers clicked over the keyboard. "Do you know the Abbott's daughter's name?"

"John didn't mention it," Viv said. "Wait. Jeff said he thought her name was Madeleine."

"I'll just key in 'Madeleine Abbott,' 'Nantucket,' and 'missing daughter.'" Lin pressed the keys and hit enter. She leaned towards the screen and scanned the multiple entries that came up about the disappearance of twenty-five years ago. She clicked on the first one and sucked in a breath when she saw the picture of the young woman staring back at them on the laptop screen. Twenty-one-year-old Madeleine Abbott had long dark brown hair just like the new ghost Lin had glimpsed behind the mansion. In the picture on the screen, the girl's bright eyes and friendly smile suggested a warm, open, outgoing personality.

Viv gazed at the girl's photograph. "She looks a lot like Amanda, doesn't she?"

Noting the resemblance, Lin's heart sank. "They could be sisters." She read the story and paraphrased for Viv. "Twenty-one-year-old Madeleine Abbott was on-island for the summer staying with her parents at the family home on Acorn Street prior to returning to Yale University in the fall for her senior year. At the time of her disappearance, Madeleine was working as a researcher for Nantucket resident Professor Anton Wilson." Lin jerked back and looked at Viv. "She was working with Anton. He knew her. Libby told him it wasn't his fault. For some reason Anton must feel responsible."

"Does the article say anything more?" Viv squinted at the screen.

Lin scooted over so Viv could get closer. She read silently and then pointed to the third paragraph of the story. "It says that Madeleine finished working at the Historical Society one evening and headed home. She briefly spoke to a friend she met on the street as she made her way to her parent's house. That was the last anyone ever saw of her."

"It's similar to Amanda's disappearance." Viv nervously rubbed her hand over her arm. "They were both walking home. It was in the evening. They look alike. They were the same age. Their bodies haven't been found." Viv shuddered. "This really freaks me out."

"Is there a link between these two cases?" Lin leaned back in her chair. "Twenty-five years apart is a long time, but...."

"But it's possible." Viv eyed her cousin. "What's this all about?"

"We need to talk to some people." Lin pulled her phone close and started to tap on her notes app. "I want to talk to the Abbotts about their daughter. I want to go to the library and look up old newspapers from the time of Madeleine's disappearance. I also think we should talk to Amanda's father. Do you think John might know where Mr. Robinson is staying? Maybe John's friend at the police station knows."

"I'll check with John."

"I'd like to bring the subject up with Anton. I wonder if he'd talk about Madeleine with me. He was visibly upset when I asked about her and what had happened."

"It's worth a try," Viv said. "See if you can talk to him the next time you work on his garden."

"There's someone else I'd like to talk to." Lin sounded hesitant.

"Who is it?"

"Kathy Lowe." Lin frowned. "But I sure don't want to question her on my own. Her comment to me about watching out for what I'm getting into has put me on edge. Will you come with me?"

Viv let out a long, loud sigh. "I'm sure not letting you go to see her alone." She narrowed her eyes. "But let me get some Mace first."

Lin started to chuckle, but her smile faded when she realized her cousin was serious. "I guess that couldn't hurt, but you could always just bring the fireplace poker along."

"It came in handy last time." Viv smiled recalling how on the last case, she ran to the backyard with the poker ready to pummel Lin's attacker.

"It certainly did." Lin hugged her cousin. Nicky showed agreement by giving a little woof. Queenie jumped onto Viv's lap and settled there.

Lin reached for the two empty teacups on the table and was about to get up to refill them when a wave of icy cold air engulfed her sending a shudder racing down her spine. She turned to look across the kitchen. Side by side near the sliding glass door to the deck, stood two ghosts, Amanda and Madeleine.

Nicky faced the spirits and let out a low, mournful whine. Queenie stood up on Viv's lap and arched her back. Viv looked from the cat to the dog to her cousin and followed their gaze. Knowing that a ghost must have appeared in the room, she spoke in a shaky voice. "Lin?"

Lin, frozen in place, gave a slight nod to Viv, but she did not move her eyes from the ghosts. The two shimmering images stared back. Their faces were serious. They didn't speak and they didn't move. They didn't need to because Lin knew why they had appeared together before her. When the ghosts were sure that Lin understood their unspoken message, their translucent forms broke into a million sparkling, swirling atoms and were gone.

Lin shivered as the chill dissipated. Viv's eyes were huge in her pale face and she took another quick glance over to the sliding doors. "A ghost?" The word came out as a whisper.

Still holding the teacups, Lin sank back down onto her chair. "They're gone."

Viv's eyebrows shot up. "There was more than one?"

"Amanda and Madeleine."

"Did they say something to you?"

"No, but I know why they came. Now I know for sure that there's definitely a connection between the girls' disappearances." Lin looked at her cousin. "And we're going to find out what it is."

CHAPTER 17

Lin walked to the reception desk of the high-end resort carrying a potted plant. She asked the man at the desk if he might ring the room of Mrs. Eleanor Abbott. Lin asked him to tell Mrs. Abbott that she knew her Realtor, John Reeves and that she hoped to speak with Mrs. Abbott if she had a few minutes. She also wanted to drop something off to apologize for her dog running onto the Abbott's property the other night.

"Mrs. Abbott will see you." The man gave Lin the number of the bungalow where Mr. and Mrs. Abbott were staying.

Lin left the main building and followed the meandering stone walkway to the bungalow area of the grounds. She admired the landscaping of greenery and flowers and the atmosphere of privacy that surrounded the grey-shingled cottages each situated with bushes and trees around them. When she saw the number she was looking for, Lin knocked on the glossy black front door.

Mrs. Abbott opened the door immediately as if

she had been perched just inside waiting for the sound of the knock. Lin almost jumped at the sudden movement of the door. Mrs. Abbott was dressed in a silk cream-colored blouse and beige linen slacks. Her hair was silvery white and looked like it had recently been done at a salon. Her makeup was professional, but understated. She smiled and gestured for Lin to enter the foyer. "Hello."

"Thank you for seeing me. I'm Carolin Coffin." Lin extended her hand and the two women shook. "This is for you and your husband." She handed Mrs. Abbott the potted plant. "My dog ran into your rear yard the other evening. I think your husband initially thought I was a prowler."

Mrs. Abbott accepted the gift and led Lin to the elegantly appointed living room where they sat down across from each other on white sofas. Lin imagined how difficult it would be to keep the light-colored furniture clean and was sure she would never sit on them if they were in her house.

Mrs. Abbott said, "Coffin. You must be related to the early founders of Nantucket?"

Lin explained that she was descended from Sebastian and Emily Coffin and that she was born on-island, but grew up in Cambridge, Massachusetts before recently returning.

"How interesting." The silver-haired woman looked eagerly at Lin. "So tell me, is there an offer on our home?"

Confusion washed over Lin and then she realized that the woman thought that she was a real estate associate of John's. "Oh, no. I'm not a Realtor. I'm a friend of John Reeves."

Mrs. Abbott's smile disappeared. "Then why did you come? Just to drop off the plant?"

"I'm sorry for the confusion. I wanted to apologize about my dog, but there is another reason that I wanted to speak with you."

Mrs. Abbott's face took on a questioning expression.

"I hoped to talk with you briefly about your daughter."

Mrs. Abbott looked like she had been slapped. She stammered before asking, "Why?"

"I hoped you might tell me about Madeleine, and the day she disappeared."

"Why on earth are you interested?" The older woman's face flushed and her cheeks turned bright red. She pressed her hands together in her lap. "Are you with law enforcement?"

"No." Lin shook her head. "I'm more of a private investigator." She chose her words carefully so that she wouldn't get into trouble for claiming to be something she wasn't.

"I don't want to talk about Madeleine." Mrs. Abbott looked like she was about to get up.

Lin said hurriedly, "There are similarities between your daughter's disappearance and the case of Amanda Robinson who has recently gone missing. I met Amanda on the night that she disappeared. I feel a duty to look into it."

"That poor girl." Mrs. Abbott choked out the words just as the front door opened and Mr. Abbott and another man walked in.

Lin recognized the man with Mr. Abbott as Ken Milliken, the president of the Abbott Group who she'd seen at the Irish pub.

"Eleanor?" Mr. Abbott wore a suit jacket, buttoned-down shirt, and tan chinos. His forehead creased with concern. He strode across the space and sat down beside his wife placing an arm over her shoulders. He gave Lin a stern look and then turned back to his wife. "What's wrong?"

"This young woman is asking questions about Madeleine." The woman could barely squeak out the words.

Graham Abbott stared at Lin, his eyes flashing with anger. "Who are you? Why are you making inquiry about our daughter?"

Ken Milliken spoke. "I'll talk to you later, Graham." He turned and left the bungalow through the front door.

Eleanor started to weep. She excused herself and headed away to the master bedroom.

Lin heard the door close. She swallowed and explained to Mr. Abbott who she was and that she'd met him when her dog ran onto his property the other night. She also explained why she had interest in his daughter's case. "I'm sorry to have upset your wife."

Abbott collected himself and shifted in his seat. "The anniversary of losing Madeleine is next week. My wife becomes very emotional at this time every year."

Lin murmured something sympathetic. She didn't want to say much until she could determine if Mr. Abbott would be willing to talk to her.

The man ran his hand through his still-thick white hair. "It's hard to believe that it's been twenty-five years." His square shoulders drooped a bit.

"What was Madeleine like?"

Abbott's face softened. "She was wonderful. Intelligent ... she was at Yale, you know. She loved history, enjoyed learning about the history of the island. She was a friendly girl, easy to know, talkative, engaging. She had a bright future ahead of her."

"I understand that she was working with Professor Anton Wilson that summer. Do you know what she was researching?"

The man's brows furrowed as he pondered. "I can't recall." He shook his head. "I should remember, but I don't know. Something about Nantucket."

"Can you tell me about her friends? Was she dating? Did she have any issues or trouble with anyone?"

"Nothing like that. She'd dated a boy at school,

but that was over before the summer began. She wasn't dating anyone at the time she went missing. She had some nice, close friends. Her best friend summered here for years since the time the girls were small. They were very close."

"What was the girl's name?"

"Audrey Mullins. She and her family never returned to the island after Madeleine went missing. We lost contact with them."

"Did Audrey attend Yale as well?"

"Cornell."

"Did you ever have a sense of what might have happened to your daughter? An instinct about who might have been involved?"

Mr. Abbott stiffened. His face hardened. Lin could see a slight twitch near the man's jaw line. "We left it in the hands of the police."

Something about the statement caused something to flicker in Lin's brain. The comment seemed off slightly, but she didn't know why. "What about you or Mrs. Abbott? Did either of you have a run-in with someone? I'm sure the police asked, but maybe over the years you've thought of something small that didn't seem right? A little thing that might seem off could lead to answers."

Daggers shot from Mr. Abbott's eyes. "Are you blaming my wife and me for Madeleine's disappearance?"

Lin leaned forward. "No, no. That isn't my intention at all. It's just that often we overlook things because they seem inconsequential when a tiny thing might shed new light on some aspect of the case."

Lin heard soft footsteps coming down the hallway. Mrs. Abbott came around the corner. Her face was drawn and her skin was blotchy. "I'm sorry for rushing away. It's just that ...." Her voice trailed off.

Lin and Mr. Abbott stood. He held his hand out to his wife and she walked over and grasped it. She took a seat on the sofa next to him. "I know that so many years have passed, but when this time of year comes along I just relive the ordeal and all those emotions resurface."

The woman's sorrow and loss caused Lin to tear up. She couldn't imagine losing a loved one like the Abbotts had, never knowing what happened to the person or where the body was. Lin thought the unknown aspect of such a situation must add another layer of horror and grief for those left behind.

Lin watched Mr. Abbott pat his wife's hand. She thought the man's movements seemed stiff and robotic and not comforting in the least.

"I'm sorry for upsetting you." Lin wanted to put an arm around the woman. "My intention is only to try and help figure things out."

"Oh, I understand, dear." Mrs. Abbott seemed about to descend into tears, but she took a deep breath and kept it together. "One never gets over a loss like this." She wrung her hands and shifted on her seat. "And that girl who came here ... oh, my."

Lin straightened. "What girl?" She wondered if Mrs. Abbott had thought of something that happened just before or after Madeleine went missing.

Mrs. Abbott lifted her eyes to Lin. "That missing girl."

Lin blinked, confused. "Do you mean Amanda Robinson?"

The older woman nodded. "It's just terrible. Another missing girl."

"Amanda Robinson came here?" Lin still wasn't sure what Mrs. Abbott meant.

"Yes. A few days before she disappeared."

Lin's heart thudded. "Why? Why did she come here?"

"She wanted to talk to me about Madeleine."

"What was her interest? How did she know about Madeleine?" Lin was dumbfounded by this bit of information.

"She said that she was studying journalism." Mrs. Abbott dabbed at her eyes with her finger. "She was particularly interested in investigative journalism. She'd heard about our family's case and was researching it. She asked about Madeleine, just like you."

A flash of anxiety washed over Lin. Amanda had come to question the Abbotts about their missing daughter and a few days later, she disappeared herself. It couldn't be a coincidence.

"Did you tell her anything you haven't told me?" Lin directed the question to the woman, but she locked eyes with Mr. Abbott.

"I told the young woman what my husband told you. I could hear you both talking while I was resting on my bed. There isn't anything else to tell, I'm afraid."

Lin wondered how accurate that statement was. "Have you told the police that Amanda was here not long before she went missing?"

"Why, no." Mrs. Abbott looked alarmed. "I didn't think it was relevant."

Lin stood up. "I think you'd better contact the police and let them know that Amanda recently spoke with you about your daughter's case." She thanked the Abbotts for their time and walked to the door. Her heart pounded crazily and a trickle of cold sweat ran down her back. *Am I in danger now for having spoken to the Abbotts about Madeleine?*

CHAPTER 18

Lin found out from John and his contact at the police station that Amanda's father, Ted Robinson, was staying at a bed and breakfast inn on a quiet side street down near the docks. She needed to talk to him about Amanda and her interest in Madeleine Abbott's disappearance twenty-five years ago. Lin worried that the man would think she was intruding and wouldn't agree to speak with her. Anxiety and nervousness buzzed through her body as she walked up the granite steps to the inn, opened the door, and stepped into a beautifully decorated foyer. When the front door opened, a little bell sounded and Lin waited for the proprietor to appear.

A short, skinny man wearing black frame glasses hurried around a corner holding a dust cloth. "Hello." He greeted Lin with a warm smile.

Lin asked about Ted Robinson explaining that she wanted to speak with him.

"Let me ring his room." The man walked over to a roll-top desk and lifted the receiver of a phone.

He punched in three numbers and waited. When a voice came on, he explained to Mr. Robinson that a young woman was in the foyer and wished to have a word with him about his daughter, Amanda. The man listened and clicked off. "He'll be right down. Would you like to sit on the back porch and wait for Mr. Robinson there? I'll bring him to you once he comes down."

Lin followed the owner of the inn down a hallway and out to a covered porch that overlooked the lush back yard. "Your landscaping is beautiful."

"My partner and I handle the gardening ourselves." The owner of the inn beamed with pride and after spending a few minutes talking with Lin about plants and garden design, he returned to the house to wait for Ted Robinson to come downstairs.

Lin took a seat in a white wicker chair and enjoyed the quiet garden. When she heard footsteps approaching, she stood up. A man in his late forties with sandy blonde hair and brown eyes stepped onto the porch and looked at Lin with a quizzical expression. His posture and energy made Lin think that this man was used to being the most powerful person in the room.

She introduced herself and offered her sympathies over the man's missing daughter. Lin had to be very careful not to slip and mention anything about seeing Amanda's spirit. The two took seats on the porch.

"I met Amanda and her boyfriend late in the evening on the day that she went missing." Lin recounted how she'd fallen on the sidewalk and how helpful Amanda had been to her. She told Mr. Robinson that she felt a duty to help find out what had happened to his daughter. "The police told you about a similar case that happened twenty-five years ago?"

Robinson's eyebrows went up. "The police didn't mention it to me. I brought it up with them. My wife knew the missing girl."

Lin's mouth opened in surprise. "So that's how Amanda knew about Madeleine Abbott."

Robinson nodded. "My wife was good friends with Madeleine. They'd spent many summers together here on the island."

"Someone told me that your wife passed away," Lin said.

"About six months ago. Losing her hit me and Amanda hard."

She didn't know why, but a twinge of distrust picked at Lin. "I'm very sorry." She leaned forward. "What was your wife's name?"

"Audrey Mullins. Audrey had spoken to Madeleine shortly before she disappeared that day twenty-five years ago. She bumped into Madeleine in town. Madeleine invited Audrey to come along with her to her house, but Audrey declined. She was tired from getting up early for work and she wanted to go home for a nap. She told Madeleine that she would come over later in the day. Audrey was the last one to have spoken with Madeleine. She was never able to shake off the guilt that she felt over the incident. Audrey always said that if she'd gone with her friend that day then nothing would have happened to her."

Lin let out a sigh. "I have similar feelings about your daughter. If I had kept taking to her longer, maybe she wouldn't have run into the person who…."

Mr. Robinson's eyes were kind. "I told my wife over and over that there wasn't anything she could have done to change things. There wasn't anything you could have done either."

"Your wife shared her experience with your daughter? That's how Amanda knew about the case?"

Robinson nodded. "Amanda wanted to do something important for her mother. She wanted to find out what happened to Madeleine. She wanted to have a hand in bringing the person to justice." The man bit his lower lip and looked out over the garden. "I never in a million years thought that Amanda would go missing … or that Brian would be killed." Robinson's body seemed to diminish as his back pressed into the seat cushion. "They were two great people. They made a nice couple. I was happy that they were together."

Lin's heart felt like a lead weight in her chest. "Do you think it's a coincidence that Amanda disappeared like Madeleine did? Or do you think that Amanda's research into the cold case was the reason for her disappearance? And Brian's murder?"

The muscles around Mr. Robinson's mouth twitched and he bit down on his lip. He kept his eyes trained on the trees at the edge of the inn's property for a full minute before he answered. "Amanda and her mother had a special bond. Amanda knew that the unsolved case weighed on Audrey all of her life. My sweet girl wanted to investigate Madeleine's disappearance as a way to honor her mother. Her desire to do something good and kind got her and Brian killed." He turned his red-rimmed eyes to Lin. "That's what I think."

With a heavy heart, Lin gave the slightest nod.

"I told the police that there might be a link between Amanda and Madeleine Abbott's disappearance. I got the feeling that they thought I was clutching at straws." He straightened. "I did hire a private investigator, but so far, he hasn't discovered a thing." Robinson turned the palms of his hands up. "I don't know what else I can do."

"Something will get uncovered." Lin tried to sound optimistic.

He shook his head and his voice was tight with emotion. "I know Amanda isn't alive. I know that she isn't coming back. I would just like to have my daughter's body. I can't stand the thought of her out there ... alone." Robinson made eye contact with Lin. “You’ve been asking around town about Amanda trying to find out what happened to her?”

“Yes. My cousin, Viv, has been helping, too.”

“Well, the two of you need to be very careful.” Worry etched over Robinson’s forehead. “If the same person is responsible for these two missing girls, then he has a lot at stake and will obviously stop at nothing to keep his secret hidden.”

Anxiety flashed through Lin’s body. She took a deep breath and tried to shake it off. Speaking with Mr. Robinson had strengthened her resolve to help solve the mystery of his missing daughter. “I only talked to Amanda for a few minutes, but I liked her immediately.” Lin smiled recalling the friendly young woman, but then her face clouded. “An evil person has stolen the lives of two fine women, and he is probably responsible for the death of Amanda’s boyfriend. I’m going to do what I can to find out who this killer is so that he can never hurt anyone ever again.”

Mr. Robinson blinked. “I hope you can do it. But please, please be careful.”

The two stood and Lin shook hands with the man.

“Keep in touch,” Mr. Robinson said.

“I promise.” Lin walked through the living room of the inn, exited the front door, and stepped down the stairs to the sidewalk. As she was turning to head home, a cold whoosh of air blew over her and she stopped. Lin looked across the street to see

Sebastian standing on the brick walkway, his form glimmering in the sunlight.

She smiled at the ghost. Sebastian stared straight-faced at Lin. She took a quick glance up and down the street and started to cross. For a moment, Sebastian turned his gaze on the inn, shook his head, and slowly faded away.

CHAPTER 19

Lin, Jeff, and John walked into town to meet Viv at the bookstore. Lin's little dog trotted alongside them. It was the yearly summer sidewalk festival and Nantucket town was buzzing with activity. Viv bustled about in front of her bookstore waiting on customers and straightening books on shelves that had been lined up outside on the sidewalk. Two of her employees held trays and offered customers free mini cups of iced coffee and tiny pastries from Viv's café.

"Looks like things are in full swing." Lin greeted her cousin with a smile.

"It's been crazy here all morning." Viv had little beads of perspiration on her forehead. "I've never seen the annual festival so busy."

"The weather couldn't be more perfect. It's drawn everyone out." Jeff held Lin's hand in his.

John gave Viv a hug and a kiss. "Maybe I'll hang around out here and pass out my business cards to people," he joked.

Jeff eyed all the customers milling around the

book shelves. "Are you able to get away?" he asked Viv. "We could just stay and help out."

Viv wiped her hands on her bartender-style apron. "Mallory's here now. She's going to hold down the fort for the afternoon." Viv often wondered how she got so lucky to have such a great employee as Mallory. "Come on, Nick," Viv called to the dog. "Queenie's inside waiting for you." Nicky followed Viv into the store where he found the cat in her usual place on the upholstered chair and jumped up to sit with her.

Viv freshened up and then returned to the sidewalk with the cat and dog following behind her. She slipped her arm through John's and led the group down the walkway into the center of town. They'd made plans to have lunch together on John's boat and then spend some time walking around the festival. John and Jeff wanted the girls to take the day off from investigating, but Lin and Viv thought it was the perfect opportunity to bump into some people they wanted to question further.

As they walked by the stores, Lin asked John, "What can you tell us about the Abbotts?" She had reported to Viv, John, and Jeff the news of her visits to the Abbotts and Mr. Robinson.

John had his arm around Viv's shoulders. "Mrs. Abbott's family has owned the mansion for years. Mr. Abbott is a businessman. He owns a company called the Abbott Group that has holdings in food distribution, restaurants, casinos, hotels. He's made a fortune. They live in New York and come here in the summers. Mrs. Abbott spends the whole summer here, but he flies back and forth and comes mostly for weekends."

"Even though their property abuts mine," Viv said, "I've never interacted with them. We have different lives and move in different social circles. I knew that years ago they'd lost a child, but I never knew the details until recently." Viv glanced at her cousin and touched her arm as they strolled along the brick sidewalk. "I can't shake the feeling that you're in danger now because you talked to the Abbotts about Madeleine. Amanda interviewed them and then she went missing. I'm not letting you out of my sight today."

Lin forced a smile. "I'm not in any danger," she tried to reassure Viv. "I just had a chat with the Abbotts, that's all. Talking to the couple isn't going to make me disappear." Lin's heart skipped a beat. She wouldn't admit that she was feeling anxious and worried because Amanda disappeared shortly after she'd spoken with the Abbotts. Lin had to focus her energy on finding the killer and not obsess about her own safety.

Jeff tightened his hold on Lin's hand. "I'm not letting you out of my sight today either."

"Nothing can happen to me now." Lin smiled. "I'm surrounded by my bodyguards."

"Do you suspect the Abbotts?" Jeff asked.

That very thought had been at the back of Lin's

mind since she met Mr. Abbott. There was something about the man that she didn't like.

"What? Mr. Abbott?" Viv nearly shouted and she clapped her hand over her mouth when she realized how loud she'd spoken. She looked over her shoulder to see if anyone was glancing her way. She lowered her voice. "You think he killed his own daughter?"

"It could have been an accident." Lin was careful to keep her voice soft. "He might have panicked and covered it up."

"Amanda comes around asking questions and Abbott kills her to keep her from snooping around," John suggested.

"Then Amanda's boyfriend tries to find out what happened to her and ends up getting killed himself." Jeff's eyes narrowed and he looked down at Lin. "You need to be watchful. Don't be alone with anyone you don't know well. Keep your phone with you at all times. Put the police on speed dial. Be careful who you trust."

Be careful who you trust. Lin shivered remembering that Liliana had said those very same words to her when she visited the older woman on her patio.

"We need to be on the lookout for people we want to talk to about Amanda," Viv said. "The dock area is where the restaurants' booths are going to be set up. It might be a good place to run into people." For a flat fee, people could buy a food pass and go from booth to booth sampling each restaurant's offerings. It was a huge hit each year and with a portion of the proceeds going to charity it raised a good deal of money for worthy causes. "After lunch, we should look for Kathy Lowe and Jessie and ask them more questions."

The four of them weaved around tourists and townsfolk stopping occasionally on the way to the boat to chat with friends and acquaintances. The fun, festive atmosphere was tainted with the thought that a killer disguised as an upstanding citizen may be lurking on the streets or passing the two couples on the sidewalks. Lin couldn't help eyeing the people they passed with suspicion.

Nantucket town had an extensive dock system where boats and yachts of all sizes were moored. The docks were always crowded with people strolling by to view the vessels. John's boat was moored on a section that led to the area where the huge yachts were docked. That part of the docks was only accessible to the owners, their guests and crews. Tourists could stand near the gate with the "Private" sign attached to it and ogle the magnificent yachts.

John often spoke with disdain about the excessive show of wealth on display at the far end of the docks and Viv always pooh-poohed him saying, "Once you make your billion in real estate, you'll have a yacht moored right next to them."

John and Viv climbed aboard his boat and Jeff

stepped on and turned to take Lin's hand. As she was reaching forward, Lin heard a voice she knew and paused. She turned around to see Mrs. Abbott wearing a big floppy hat. The woman was heading to the yachts and was chattering away with a companion when Lin called to her.

Mrs. Abbott blinked and then recognized Lin. "Miss Coffin. Hello, dear."

Lin stepped closer to the two women and Mrs. Abbott introduced Lin to her friend. The other woman said, "Are you the gardener?"

Lin nodded.

"My sister is a client of yours. She raves about you. Are you taking new business, by any chance? My garden is in a shambles."

When Lin told Mrs. Abbott's friend that she would be able to fit her into the schedule, the woman practically hugged her. They made arrangements for Lin to come by the property and discuss the woman's needs.

Just as they were about to part ways, Lin spoke to Mrs. Abbott. "Could I talk to you for a minute?" Lin glanced at the friend.

Mrs. Abbott said to her companion, "I'll meet you on the boat."

The friend smiled and headed away down the dock to the Abbott's yacht.

"What is it, my dear?"

"I just have a quick question for you. When Amanda came to talk to you, were you alone? Was anyone else in the bungalow when you met with her? A friend, the housekeeper, Mr. Abbott?"

"I was alone with Amanda. Of course, later on I told my husband and several friends about her visit. Why do you ask?"

"I just wondered who else might have known that Amanda had spoken with you." Lin smiled trying to seem casual. "Just covering all the bases."

"Is this yours?" Mrs. Abbott gestured to John's boat.

"Oh, no. It belongs to my friend." Lin introduced Mrs. Abbott to Viv, Jeff, and John who were standing aft.

"Mrs. Abbott, did Amanda ask you anything that I didn't? Did she bring anything up that I didn't?" Lin had been wondering if Amanda had stumbled across something that indicated she was getting too close to discovering who caused Madeleine's disappearance.

The older woman's lips pursed and her forehead crinkled as she thought back on her meeting with the young woman. She shrugged a shoulder. "Nothing I can think of."

Lin smiled again reassuringly. "I just wondered. It's nice to see you again."

"You must visit us on our boat sometime." Mrs. Abbott waved in the direction of the private dock.

"Is Mr. Abbott joining you today?"

"He's on board already. We're hosting several friends for lunch and then we're going to stroll around the festival. I'd better get going."

"Enjoy the day."

Mrs. Abbott hurried away.

CHAPTER 20

The foursome sat around the table under the boat's awning finishing their lunches of green salad, pasta salad, and grilled panini sandwiches. Viv had brought out sliced fresh fruit for dessert and iced tea with lemon. Conversation was light and easy and steered clear of the subject of missing persons. Queenie and Nicky were curled up on the deck in the sun, snoozing. Tourists strolling past on the docks glanced at the two young couples enjoying each other's company and never guessed that the weight of two mysteries was pressing down on them.

Viv stood up. "We need to start walking around. I have to get back to the bookstore in a while."

"Can't you take the day off from investigating?" John asked.

Viv picked up some dirty plates from the table. "No." She headed below to the galley.

John groaned and shuffled his feet to stand.

"Why don't you two stay here and relax," Lin suggested. "Viv and I will stroll around together for a little while."

Jeff frowned. "We should go along with you."

"There's no need." Lin smiled. "It's broad daylight and there must be a million people at the festival. Nothing can happen to us."

Viv came back up on deck. "Anyway, no one will ever talk to us if two good-looking guys are standing there with us."

Nicky stretched and jumped down.

"I have my guard dog with me, too." Lin bent and scratched the little creature's ears.

"You have your phone?" Jeff asked.

Lin held it up. "Right here. We'll be back before you know it."

Nicky and the girls left the boat and headed down the docks to the food festival section. Viv whispered, "The guys clucking and fussing over us gets me all nervous and scared."

"Really?" Lin elbowed her cousin playfully. "I thought you got that way all on your own."

The girls spotted the booth for the Irish pub and saw Kathy Lowe setting out desserts on the counter. Kathy noticed Lin and Viv and scowled at them.

"Maybe we should avoid her for now." Viv pushed a stray strand of hair out of her eyes with shaky fingers. "She frightens me."

"How will we find out anything if we avoid everyone who might be the killer?"

Someone called Lin's name and the girls turned to see the Abbotts and their friends including the president of the Abbott Group, Ken Milliken, coming up behind them. "Miss Coffin," Mrs. Abbott called out. "This is Ken Milliken, a friend and business associate of ours."

Milliken was in his mid to late-forties and was trim and fit. "Your name came up at lunch. Several people praised your gardening and landscaping skills."

The woman who earlier asked Lin to take her on as a client came up beside Mrs. Abbott and hooked her arm through hers. "Ken can't be left out, you know," she said to Lin. "He has to keep up with the Joneses." The woman chuckled. "He wants nothing but the best." The two older women strolled away. Mr. Abbott stood talking to some other men and shot the girls an unfriendly glance.

Milliken said with a broad smile, "I don't see anything wrong with wanting the best."

Lin waited to hear what he wanted from her.

"I have a large place on the ocean near Madaket. It desperately needs landscaping. I'd like to hire you for the job."

"But you haven't seen any of my work."

"The comments people made at lunch are good enough for me. What do you say?"

Something about Milliken put Lin off. He was certainly friendly enough, but there was an edge to him that she didn't care for. She wondered if maybe it came from him always getting his way. "I could come out and take a look. See what you have in mind."

Milliken fished a business card out of his wallet and handed it to Lin. "I hear you're asking around about Madeleine Abbott's disappearance."

Lin was surprised by the comment. "Well, it started with me asking around about Amanda Robinson's disappearance."

Milliken ignored Lin's statement. "I knew Madeleine. We were close in age, hung around in the same group for a few summers."

"Did you know Audrey Mullins?"

Milliken raised his eyebrows. "Sure. She was Madeleine's best friend. You know Audrey? I haven't seen her for probably twenty-five years."

"I met Audrey's daughter," Lin said. "Amanda Robinson."

Milliken's face was blank and then his eyes widened. "The missing girl? She's Audrey's daughter?"

"What was your impression at the time?" Lin questioned. "Did the kids you hung out with have ideas about what happened to Madeleine?"

Just then Mr. Abbott called to Ken Milliken. "We're heading back to the boat. You want to join us for a drink?"

Ken nodded and looked at Lin. "Give me a call about the landscaping." He shook her hand and followed after Mr. Abbott and the other men.

Viv's nose crinkled like she'd smelled something bad. "I don't like him. Don't go to his place alone."

"I'll have Leonard with me." Lin watched the men walking down the dock. "Why don't you like him?"

Viv frowned. "I don't know. He acts entitled. And why did he bring up Madeleine out of the blue?"

A shiver rushed down Lin's spine. "That's a very good question."

"You want to keep walking around?"

Lin nodded and the cousins headed along the walkway of restaurant booths. Lin wanted to talk to Kathy Lowe again, but for now they steered clear of her and the Irish pub booth. "It might be worth talking to that bartender who works at the pub again. He and Madeleine Abbott were about the same age. Maybe he hung around with the same group. He might have some insight."

"I haven't seen Amanda's friend, Jessie, yet." Viv scanned the crowd. "Maybe she isn't working the event."

Something caught Lin's eye as they walked and she did a double-take at a figure sitting on a bench under a large tree next to the sidewalk. She touched Viv's arm and nodded her head in the direction of the bench.

Viv followed her cousin's gaze. "Leonard?"

The girls walked over to find the man slumped on the seat, clutching a bottle of whiskey in a paper bag, his eyes closed. Lin reached over and gently touched his shoulder. Her voice was soft.

"Leonard."

"Ruh?" Leonard grunted and opened his eyes into slits. He shifted on the bench, his movement loose and sloppy.

Lin removed the bottle from his hand and passed it to Viv who carried it to the trash receptacle. "You can't drink in public," Lin told him. "You'll end up in jail overnight again."

Leonard's eyelids fluttered. He shaded them with his meaty hand. "Why you here, Coffin?" he slurred.

"The real question is ... why are you here? Like this?"

Leonard's chin fell onto his chest.

"What are we going to do with him?" Viv looked at the drunken man. "Should I go get John and Jeff?"

Nicky jumped up on the bench and slurped his tongue over Leonard's cheek. Leonard roused. "You brought this cur with you again?" he mumbled.

Nicky lay across the man's lap and Leonard stroked the dog's fur.

Lin said, "I'll sit here with him in case the police come by. Would you ask Jeff to go get my truck and come pick us up?" She handed Viv the keys to her truck.

"Sure thing." Viv hurried away towards John's boat.

Lin settled next to Leonard on the bench. The

smell of alcohol was strong.

"Why do you do this? Get yourself into trouble?" Lin didn't use an accusatory or berating tone. She just really wanted to know.

Leonard blinked and squinted. He kept stroking the fur on Nicky's back. "I miss my wife."

When Lin asked, she really didn't expect an answer to her question and she sure didn't expect to hear Leonard speak of his wife. The sadness in his voice tugged at her heart.

"She died this time of year. I always fall into a mess around this time. That's why."

Lin asked softly, "What happened to her?"

"Car accident ... on the mainland."

"I'm sorry." A small sigh escaped her throat. "What was her name?"

"Marguerite."

"What a lovely name."

"She was a lovely person." Leonard's chin hit his chest again.

Lin looked at him. He had a scruffy shadow of facial hair showing and he smelled like he'd been sleeping in a pig-sty. "I don't think she'd want you to be unhappy."

"I know." Leonard didn't open his eyes.

"I'm going to take you back to your house. Jeff went to get the truck."

"Okay."

"I got us two new clients today. They're rich."

"You know how to pick 'em, Coffin."

Lin smiled just as Jeff pulled up to the curb in her beat-up, old junk of a truck. Jeff got out and walked to the bench where he gently slipped his hand under Leonard's arm and lifted him up. He maneuvered him into the passenger seat. "I'll take him home."

Nicky jumped in and climbed on Leonard's lap.

"I'll come, too." Lin squeezed Jeff's hand.

"Viv ran into Libby and Anton. They're sitting in front of the Whaling Museum. They want to talk to you."

"Oh." A cold bead of sweat rolled down Lin's back.

CHAPTER 21

Lin hurried along the sidewalks to the Whaling Museum wondering what Libby and Anton wanted or what they'd found out. Coming around the corner and looking over the heads of people strolling along, Lin could see them sitting on the bench outside the museum. They looked up as she approached.

"Carolin." Libby smiled. "Come sit with us." She slid to her right to make a place for Lin to sit between her and Anton. Libby patted the space with her hand.

"Have you found out anything about Amanda Robinson's murder?" Anton was wearing sunglasses and a golf shirt. Lin thought he looked surprisingly stylish and cool.

"I think her disappearance is linked to the missing person's case from twenty-five years ago." Lin realized she'd left her own sunglasses on John's boat and she wished she had them as the sun was hitting her right in the eyes, causing her to squint.

"Madeleine Abbott." Libby nodded. "We think

so, too."

Lin always felt a step or two behind Anton and Libby. "Why didn't you tell me?"

"We've just come to that conclusion." Anton let out a sigh. "We wanted to know if you agreed."

"What about suspects?" Libby kept her voice down.

"I wonder about Graham Abbott. He gives off something that makes me nervous. Viv and I also get weird vibes from the girl who works at the Irish pub, Kathy Lowe. She told me to be careful what I was stepping into. She makes me uncomfortable."

Libby shifted slightly on the bench so that the sun wasn't directly in her eyes. "Amanda must have discovered something that frightened the killer. She must have been close to figuring it out. She must have told her boyfriend her ideas or he found the clues after Amanda went missing. I wonder how the killer knew that the young people were getting close. Amanda must have been confiding in someone about her discoveries and either that person is the killer or that person revealed the information to the killer."

Lin realized she hadn't given that aspect of the case much attention and berated herself for not thinking it through as it could be very helpful in determining suspects.

"Have you seen the ghosts recently?" Libby questioned.

I haven't seen Madeleine or Amanda, but I saw

Sebastian right after I spoke with Amanda's father at the inn down near the docks. He just looked at me for a minute and then he was gone."

Anton stood up abruptly. "I need to make a call. I'll be back." He strode off down the side street.

"What's wrong with him?" Lin turned to Libby.

"In your sleuthing you must have learned that Anton had employed Madeleine Abbott as a research assistant? They'd been working together for about a month that summer when Madeleine let Anton know that she had a crush on him."

Lin's eyes went wide. "Oh."

"In fact, she made the revelation to Anton the very same day that she went missing. They were working in the historical museum together. Madeleine tried to take Anton's hand. She said she'd fallen in love with him. As you can imagine, Anton was horrified. He couldn't imagine what he'd done to encourage the girl's feelings." Libby watched the tourists for a few moments. "He became stern with Madeleine, told her it was completely inappropriate. He said he didn't think they could work together any longer. Anton did not handle it well. Madeleine got teary-eyed and hurried away." A sad frown formed over Libby's face. "Anton feels responsible for what occurred. If the incident didn't happen or he had handled it more delicately... those are his words ... then Madeleine would have remained in the museum for a few more hours. Anton believes that she would have avoided the killer and would still be alive."

"She might still have come in contact with the killer," Lin said. "It isn't Anton's fault."

"Tell that to Anton." Libby gave a weak smile. "I have for twenty-five years."

Lin sighed. "There's a lot of guilt going around."

"That is an emotion that is unhelpful and useless."

"Tell that to those of us who feel guilty." Lin held her hands in her lap.

They sat quietly until Libby broke the silence. "How's Leonard?"

Lin was surprised. She told the older woman how she'd found him drunk on a bench and had arranged for Jeff to take him home.

"Thank you. Keep your eye on him when you can. This will pass and he'll be fine again."

"How's Liliana?" Lin asked.

"She is slowly disappearing. It won't be long before she crosses over." Libby stood. "I'm going to find Anton. Let me know if you learn any more about the case." As she walked away, she said, "Be careful who you trust, Carolin."

Even as a shiver of anxiety tingled her skin, Lin rolled her eyes. She was really starting to dislike that phrase.

***

WALKING THROUGH town on her way

home, Lin received a text from Jeff reporting that he and Nicky had safely delivered Leonard to his home. Jeff left her truck in her driveway and he'd fed the dog and locked him in the house.

Lin confirmed the bike-beach trip tomorrow that they'd planned with Jeff's older sister and her husband. She was looking forward to spending the day with the three of them and having a break from the details of the case.

The sun was setting when Lin arrived home and when she opened the front door her little brown dog did a welcoming dance. Lin laughed and patted him. Her stomach was growling as she headed to the kitchen. Checking her fridge, she took out a frozen burger and thawed it in the microwave. She made a quick salad and warmed some leftover rice while the burger was broiling.

When everything was ready, she carried her meal outside to the table on her deck. It was a dark night with no moonlight. She lit the candle in the center of the wooden table and let out a contented sigh. She loved the house that her grandfather had left her and she counted her blessings as she sank into the cushions of the deck chair. The night air was warm and pleasant, she was enjoying a delicious meal, and she had her dog-buddy with her. She decided that the only thing that would make the evening even nicer was if Jeff was sitting next to her.

Her front doorbell rang just as she was lifting the

burger to her lips for another bite. Her hands froze in place. Not understanding why, a sense of cold dread washed over her and she didn't want to answer the door.

Nicky let out a nervous whine.

Lin looked at the dog sitting in the chair next to her and she placed her trembling index finger to her lips. "Shh. Don't bark," she whispered. "I don't want anyone to know we're here." She waited and almost jumped from the chair when the bell rang a second time. Someone knocked hard against the front door. "Who can it be so late? If it was Viv or Jeff, they would have texted me before showing up."

Nicky searched his owner's face.

"Maybe whoever it is will go away," Lin told him. She and the dog waited in their seats, listening.

Another hard knock sounded on the door. Lin stood. "I guess they aren't going away." She lifted the sharp knife from her dinner plate and slipped it into her back pocket. "Let's go see." She and the dog walked from the deck into the living room and quietly shuffled to the front door.

Lin sucked in a deep breath to try and steady her voice. "Who is it?"

"It's Kathy Lowe," the woman said from the other side of the door.

Lin's heart started to hammer double-time. "What do you want? I got home late. I'm having dinner."

"Open up, will you?" Kathy's voice held a tone of urgency. "I need to talk to you."

Lin hesitated then looked down at the dog. "Let's keep on our toes. Don't leave me alone with her." She opened the door.

Kathy abruptly pushed past Lin and entered the small entryway. "It took you long enough to answer." Worry pinched her face.

Lin took a quick look outside before she closed and locked the door. "What's up? Why are you here? How'd you find me?"

"It wasn't hard." Kathy moved into the living room. "Can we talk in here? I don't want to stay long."

"Sure. Do you want something to drink?"

Kathy shook her head. "It's not a social call." She sat down, but perched on the edge of the chair as if she might have to rush away at a moment's notice. "It's about Amanda."

Whatever Kathy was giving off made Lin flush with anxiety. "What about her?" Lin asked warily. She could feel the pressure of the knife in her back pocket.

"We used to talk at work. I can't stand most of the people there, but Amanda was smart, we had good conversations."

Lin waited.

"Amanda told me she was investigating an old case. She didn't give me many details, but she did mention that she needed to solve it for her mother's sake. One day, she came in and said things were starting to add up. She seemed nervous, worried. I told her if she'd found out something she should go to the police with it. She said she was going to take him down before he could stop her." Kathy shivered. "It scared me. Then she went missing ... and her boyfriend got killed. I was ready to leave the island. I was afraid that whoever hurt them would think that Amanda had confided in me. I'm still afraid. You need to figure it out."

"Did Amanda say anything at all about who the killer might be?" Lin clasped her hands together so they wouldn't shake.

Kathy shook her head and then she looked at Lin. "She only said that she hadn't wanted to believe her mother's suspicions, but her mother was right all along."

Bits of information swirled in Lin's head so fast that it almost made her dizzy. "Did she say anything else? Did she tell you any little thing that didn't seem relevant, but that might help?"

Kathy's eyes darted about the room. "I can't think of anything." She stood up. "I need to go. I don't want anyone to know I was here." She started for the door. "Amanda said that her mother warned her to be careful who she trusted."

Lin's head buzzed. *That phrase again.* She reached to her neck and ran her fingers over her horseshoe necklace.

"Her mother was right." Kathy unlocked the

front door and opened it. "Figure it out, will you? Help put the monster behind bars. Otherwise, I'm leaving Nantucket." She hurried down the steps and disappeared into the darkness.

CHAPTER 22

Lin, Jeff, Jeff's sister, Dana, and her husband, Andrew, rode their bicycles up the hill for the last few miles of their thirty-mile bike ride. They'd left early in the morning and they'd cycled at a fast pace for most of the ride that weaved along ocean vistas, past groves of trees, and alongside farms and meadows. The day was sunny and hot, but without the oppressive humidity of the past week. At the top of the hill, they followed the curving dirt road lined with short plants and scrub bushes until they reached the small parking lot.

"The beauty of bikes," Andrew said to his companions, "is we don't have to worry about finding a parking space."

The group dismounted and linked and locked the four bicycles together. Dana removed the picnic lunches from the carriers on the back of her and Andrew's bikes and the four headed to the beach with Lin carrying two small blankets she had stored in her bicycle pannier bags.

Walking along the path that was cut through the

white sand dunes, they emerged onto the beach to see the sparkling blue ocean stretched out before them. Good-sized waves crashed against the shore. People sunned themselves on their blankets and others jumped and swam and rode the swells of the sea. Lin couldn't wait to strip off her sweaty shorts and tank top, change into her swimsuit, and leap straight into the refreshing surf. They changed their clothes in the port-o-potties, put their things on the blankets, and raced each other into the water.

After an hour of body-surfing and floating on their backs, the couples plopped onto the blankets and dried themselves off in the warm sun. Dana distributed sandwiches and put out baby carrots, slices of red pepper and cucumbers and a pot of hummus to dip the veggies in. Everyone was starving from the morning of exercise and they dug into the tasty food. After eating, the guys decided to take a walk along the beach. The girls declined the invitation to join them in favor of chatting together while resting in the sun. Although Dana was fifteen years older than her brother, the two were close and she was very happy to have Jeff back on the island. She and her husband were accountants who ran their own business from Nantucket.

One of the lifeguards was returning to his post with a bottle of water he'd just purchased at the small snack stand and he nodded to Lin and Dana as he passed them. Lin recognized him as the bartender at the Irish pub. The girls waved.

"You know him?" Lin asked.

"Yeah, he's been lifeguarding here for years."

"He's a busy man. I met him at the Irish pub in town." Lin rubbed some sunscreen on her legs. "My cousin and I chatted with him the other night when we were there."

"He's a good guy. I've known him since we were in our late teens." Dana laughed. "*That* was a long time ago."

Lin capped the tube of lotion and passed it to Dana. She realized that Jeff's sister would have been close in age to Madeleine Abbott, so she asked if she'd known her.

Dana was about to pour lotion onto her palm, but she stopped and looked at Lin. She didn't speak for a few seconds. "I knew her. And what happened to her was a defining moment of my life."

Lin stared, her eyes wide.

"When Madeleine went missing, I was stunned. I realized how short and unpredictable life could be. I decided to live my life so I would have few regrets. I wanted to be as kind and happy and gentle and loving as I could be." Dana smiled. "I don't always achieve those things, but I try."

"I've only met you three times, but I'd say you definitely achieved being that kind of person." Lin gave Dana a warm, sincere smile. "You know about the girl that recently went missing?"

Dana swallowed and nodded.

"There are similarities between the cases."

Dana's face blanched. "You think it's the same person who's responsible? It's been what, twenty-five years?"

"I think it's the same person."

Dana dropped the tube of sunscreen.

"When Madeleine disappeared, did you or your friends suspect anyone?"

A bead of sweat traced along Dana's temple. She stared at the sand. "I wish there was someone who stood out. The people we hung out with had lots of opinions, though none of them were worth anything." She made eye contact with Lin. "You know, there are plenty of ghost stories about the island? Some kids thought a ghost had killed her." She snorted. "Some said an old boyfriend had come to the island to hurt her for dropping him."

"You think that was possible?"

Dana gave a weary smile. "No, it was just people grasping at any idea. I had no guess who could have done it. I was just shaken to the core that this could have happened in our town, on our island. It was something that happened in other places, not here." She looked out over the water. "We found out that summer that terrible things can happen anywhere."

"You knew Ken Milliken? He hung out in your group?"

Dana smiled. "I knew him. He did well, didn't

he?" She shook her head. "We weren't friends, but we hung out in the same group sometimes."

"What did you think of him?"

"Ken was very ambitious, hardworking. His desire to make it in the world practically poured out of him. It put me off. He had an edge that I didn't like."

"A dangerous edge?"

Dana tilted her head in thought. "I didn't sense that in him, but his drive for money and position seemed to consume him. You know, I read an article not too long ago that reported that a huge percentage of CEOs have sociopathic tendencies ... not killers or anything, but no remorse for things they do, no empathy for others, things like that. When I read it, I immediately thought of Ken."

Lin shook her head, disgusted.

Dana went on. "I doubt he'll be content with being president of the Abbott Group for long. I'm sure he has much bigger ambitions."

"Was he friends with Madeleine?"

"Not really friends. I always thought he had a crush on her. He kept his distance though. I think her family's wealth made him think he had no business with her."

Lin thought about that comment. Would being poor have made Ken angry because he wasn't worthy of Madeleine? Would it have made him want to take what he couldn't have? Anxiety flitted over her skin. "I have an appointment to meet with

Ken tomorrow. He wants to hire me for some landscaping work."

"Well, don't go out there alone," Dana said only half-joking. "It's an isolated property, used to be a farm. It's been in his family for generations." Dana leaned back a bit on the blanket and stretched her legs out in front of her. "There was something about Madeleine. She was pretty, yes, but it was her personality. She was fun to be around. She had an energy that was infectious, she drew you in." Dana ran her hand over the warm sand. "She had a lot of guys interested in her."

"I heard that Madeleine had broken up with her boyfriend at Cornell. Was she interested in anyone on-island that summer?"

Dana shook her head. "She wasn't. Guys asked her out. She never went. She was serious about the research work she was doing."

Lin thought about how Madeleine had developed a crush on Anton Wilson, an intelligent, successful, dapper professor. None of the young men her own age could compete with that.

"Who else was interested in Madeleine?"

"Oh, gee, let me think. There was a guy who ended up marrying Madeleine's friend, Audrey. The guy had a thing for Madeleine that summer."

"Ted Robinson?" Lin was surprised by the information.

Dana's eyebrows shot up. "How do you know him?"

Lin leveled her eyes at the woman sitting next to her. "The missing girl, Amanda Robinson. Ted is her father."

Dana's hand flew to her mouth. "What an awful coincidence."

"Ted liked Madeleine?"

"Yeah." Dana nodded. "I didn't know him well. Just in passing. Someone told me that summer that he wanted to date Madeleine."

"Then he ends up marrying her friend."

"Maybe the adversity brought them together."

"Audrey passed away not too long ago."

"Did she? That's too bad. She would have been around my age, mid-forties. Do you know how she died?"

"I didn't hear." Lin spotted Jeff and Andrew returning from their walk.

As they approached the blanket, Jeff said to the girls. "We're hot. We need another swim. You want to come in with us?" He knelt next to Lin and gave her a sweet kiss.

She smiled and stood up. "Race you." She took off towards the waves with the others running right behind her.

CHAPTER 23

Lin shifted in the driver's seat. Despite putting on tons of sunscreen the previous day, she'd managed to get a slight burn on her back. Nicky had his paws on the armrest of the passenger seat and was straining to get his nose up to the small opening in the window. Nerves jangled through Lin's body as she pulled into the long, winding driveway and maneuvered the truck along the road passing fields and trees and stonewalls.

Though it was a lovely setting, Lin couldn't enjoy the view since she was feeling unsettled and distrustful about meeting Ken Milliken at his home to discuss the landscaping he wanted done. Up ahead, Lin saw a beautiful, restored Colonial farmhouse standing at the end of the driveway. Leonard was going to meet her, but she didn't see his truck and her heart dropped. Lin pulled her truck to a stop in front of a huge red barn and stepped out. As she was letting Nicky out of the passenger side, Milliken emerged from the house and called out a greeting. Lin thought it odd that he was dressed in a suit and tie.

"You found it okay, I see." Milliken shook her hand.

"No trouble. It's a beautiful piece of land." Lin glanced around. She wished Leonard would show up.

Milliken looked down at the little brown dog sitting at Lin's feet.

"I hope you don't mind my dog."

"It's fine." His facial expression didn't match his words. "This was my grandparent's farm." He chuckled. "Obviously, farming wasn't for me. I sold off most of the land to developers, kept ten acres for myself and this house and outbuildings."

Lin thought he must have made a fortune selling off so much land. She also thought that his grandfather wouldn't have been happy about it.

The sound of an engine caused the two to turn towards the driveway. Leonard's truck bounced around the corner and came to a halt.

Lin breathed a sigh of relief.

Nicky darted over to welcome the man. Leonard got out of his vehicle and bent to scratch the dog's ears. He walked over to Lin and Milliken. "Mornin.'"

Milliken took the landscapers on a tour of the property around the house, outlining what he wanted done. The three went to sit on the front porch where Milliken had a leather portfolio set on the wooden table. He showed Lin and Leonard pictures he'd found in architectural magazines and on the internet of what he wanted done with the grounds. "There's an addition to the house planned to start in a few weeks. I don't have enough room to entertain the way the house is now. The kitchen was redone a year ago, but I've changed my mind about the space and that will be renovated as well."

Lin looked over the photographs that Milliken pushed toward her and passed them to Leonard.

"A swimming pool and a hot tub are going in soon, too." He handed them blueprint copies of both the house and pool plans. "I'd like these areas to be extensively landscaped." He ran his finger over the blueprints.

Lin blinked at the man's requests. "You understand we aren't a large landscaping firm?"

Milliken looked blankly at her.

"What Lin is telling you is that we're a small operation." Leonard gestured towards the blueprints. "What you want will take a larger-scale operation than what we can manage."

Milliken scoffed. "I'm told you're the best and I want the best." He moved his hand in a wide arc. "Then expand your operation."

After more back and forth discussion, it was agreed that Lin and Leonard would take the information back with them and would go over it to consider if it was a job they could handle.

"We do have other clients," Lin told the man. "I'm just not sure we can handle this to everyone's satisfaction."

Milliken stood up and walked them to their trucks. "As I said, perhaps it's time for you to expand. Now is the time. The demand is obviously there."

Lin looked around for her dog. "Did you see where Nicky went?" She turned in a circle and called for the creature.

"He's probably investigating." Leonard set off for the rear yard with Lin and Milliken following. The dog was nowhere to be seen.

Lin's heart beat sped up. The dog never ran off like this. "Nicky! Nick!" Panic gripped her.

Leonard heard the alarm in the young woman's voice. "We'll find him, Coffin."

As they were about to walk around to the far corner of the farmhouse, a woof was heard behind them and Lin rushed in the direction of the sound.

The backyard near the house was flat and level and then the lawn gently sloped downhill to the part of the property that led to thick woods. The beginning of a trail could be seen in the opening of a stone wall and the little brown dog stood looking up the hill at them. His stub of a tail was twitching wildly from side to side. He woofed, turned, and darted into the trees. Lin took a quick glance at Leonard and took off after the dog.

"You're going after him?" Milliken frowned and glanced at his watch. "I have to get to another meeting in town."

Lin reached the bottom of the hill and ran along the trail. She could hear Leonard crashing behind her. "Nick!"

She ran for some distance and at last saw the dog standing at the edge of a small clearing. He turned his head to Lin and barked again.

Lin stood at the entrance to the small meadow. Leonard lurched up to her breathing hard. "What's wrong with that crazy mutt? You got a leash to put on him?"

When Lin didn't answer, the man took a look at her face. "What's wrong with you, Coffin?"

Lin's face was white. "He never does this. Something's wrong." Her voice was soft. She pulled her phone from her back pocket. Her hand was so wet with sweat that it almost slipped from her hand. "Come on."

She took a few steps into the field before Leonard moved to follow her. When she reached the other side of the grassy clearing, the dog gave her a quick glance and whined. Nicky's eyes were glued to a spot between two huge trees. Lin sucked in a breath just as Leonard came up beside her. Her vision was spinning so fast that she reached over and gripped the man's arm.

A small depression could be seen hidden under some leaves and dirt. Nicky ran to the spot and howled, his nose pointing to the sky. Lin's legs gave out and Leonard helped her slide down to the grass.

***

THE POLICE were called to investigate what turned out to be a recent grave dug into the spot between the trees. Using the clothing the body had been wearing, the preliminary determination was that Amanda Robinson was buried there. Ken Milliken was taken into custody for questioning.

After two hours of talking to the police and the detectives, and needing some time to regain her equilibrium, Lin and Nicky climbed into the truck and drove slowly home with Leonard following behind in his own vehicle. Lin parked in her driveway and Leonard walked her to the door of her small house.

"At least the girl can rest in peace now." He held Lin's elbow as she walked up the few steps to the landing.

Lin nodded. "There's still so much to figure out."

"The police will get to the bottom of it. It'll be okay. You want me stay for a while?"

"I'll be fine." Lin managed a weak smile. She looked down at her sweet brown dog. "I'm going to go cook up some steak for the little hero who found the body." She swung her front door open. "I'll see you tomorrow."

Leonard gave a nod, went to his truck, and drove away.

Lin made Nicky a beef dinner and he gobbled the

food as fast as he could chew. She called Viv to report on what had happened and then decided to go rest on her bed. In two minutes, she had fallen asleep.

After a two-hour nap, Lin showered, made a sandwich and sat down at the kitchen island to answer emails while she ate. Her mind returned to the awful discovery made hours earlier on Ken Milliken's property. Although she was grateful that Amanda's body had finally been found, anxiety still coursed through her veins. *What about Madeleine? Is Milliken responsible for her death, too?* Thoughts spun around in Lin's brain. Something was wrong. She was missing something.

But what?

CHAPTER 24

Lin worked for several hours at her laptop doing some programming for the Boston company she worked for remotely. She needed something to focus on other than the disappearances and crimes that had taken over her life for the past couple of weeks. Still unable to shake off the disturbing feeling that something was wrong, Lin talked herself into believing that it was just a normal reaction to what had happened and that she would need some time for her emotions to settle down.

She changed into shorts and a tank top and decided to go for an evening run around the streets on the outskirts of town. The rhythmic motion calmed her nerves and cleared her head and after five miles of slow jogging she returned to her house feeling much better.

After her third shower of the day, Lin picked up her phone to call the inn near the docks where Ted Robinson was staying. She wanted to offer her condolences to him and tell him that she was relieved that now he could bring his daughter home. The innkeeper picked up the call and rang Mr. Robinson's room, but no one answered. Just as Lin clicked off, her phone buzzed with an incoming text from Viv.

John's friend from the police station said that Ken Milliken isn't the killer. Milliken was off-island in New York City on the weekend that Amanda disappeared. He was attending a relative's wedding.

Lin stared at her phone screen stunned by the news that Milliken was innocent. She sat down at the kitchen table and put her head in her hands. Thoughts raced through her mind like water swirling out of a sieve, each piece of information from the case like a separate drop of liquid that spilled out in every direction.

Suddenly a thought popped up. It was vague and unformed, but the little spark in her brain caused her to slide her laptop over in front of her. She opened it and tapped on the keys, her heart pounding with anticipation. After putting the words into the search bar and hitting enter, several entries came up and she clicked on one of them. She read the article and sucked in a sharp breath. *Oh, my God.*

For a moment she looked across the room, thinking, and then she reread the article. Her body went rigid and her breathing was rapid and shallow. *Be careful who you trust.*

Lin's doorbell rang causing her to jump to her

feet with surprise. She pushed her hair out of her eyes as she hurried to the door expecting Viv to be standing there on the front landing. Her eyes went wide when she saw who was there in the darkness.

"May I come in?" Ted Robinson asked. "I've heard from the police."

"I, ah...." Lin stammered. Her face was white.

Robinson stepped around Lin and into the entryway. He closed the door behind him. "I'd like to thank you for all you did to help find my daughter. I'm on my way to the police station. I'll only stay a second."

Robinson walked into the living room and sat down. Lin took the chair by the door to the deck.

"Are you all right?" Robinson asked.

Lin stared at him. "I'm shook up by it all."

"I am as well." He glanced around the room. "The police said your dog led you to the grave. Is he here?"

Lin flicked her eyes to the kitchen. Nicky stood in the doorway, the ruff of fur on his back standing up straight.

Robinson saw the animal and looked almost relieved. "This little guy? Well." He turned his eyes back to Lin and his face hardened. His hands gripped the arms of the chair. His breathing was coming in short puffs.

Lin knew she was right. Robinson was the killer. She glared at him. "Your wife."

"What about her?" the man sneered. His eyes

bulged and his jaw went slack. He seemed to have morphed into a monster.

"She died." Lin could barely get the words out of her mouth. "In your hot tub?"

"My wife didn't know how to swim." A crooked smile formed on Robinson's face.

"Audrey figured it out, didn't she? She figured out that you killed Madeleine Abbot. You couldn't have that bit of information come out about you, could you? The big CEO. The big, important man." Lin choked on her words. "So you killed your wife to silence her." Lin had the sensation of ice water filling up her throat. She could barely breathe. "Amanda found out what your wife suspected about you. So you killed Amanda. Your own daughter." Tears spilled from Lin's eyes.

"Amanda wouldn't listen to me. I told her Audrey was wrong. I told her that she and her mother had it all wrong. I told her that I could explain. She wouldn't believe me. I hate it when people won't listen to me." Robinson's face was beet-red. His wild eyes roved about the room. "I…." He looked down at his hands. "She wouldn't stop saying that I was a killer … so I made her stop. I put my hands on her neck." His hands balled into fists as he slowly raised his eyes to Lin. "I talked to Brian. I wasn't sure what he knew, so I had to do it. I asked him to meet me on Tangerine Street. I told him I was going to rent the house over there. He agreed to come when I said I had information about

Amanda and where she was." Robinson shrugged. "Brian believed me. He had to die. I can't have people spreading rumors about me."

Lin shuddered. Her head was spinning. She had to get out of the house. She started to gag and pushed herself out of her chair.

Robinson lunged at her.

Nicky flew at the man and sank his teeth into his leg just as the front door flew open. Leonard charged into the room and tackled Ted Robinson to the floor.

***

"**THAT'S THE** second time you came to my rescue." Lin smiled wearily.

"You can't seem to stay out of trouble, Coffin."

They were sitting on Lin's deck with the roof's floodlight illuminating the yard. Lin and Leonard had spent a good amount of time recounting their stories to the police. Ted Robinson had been hauled off to the station where he would soon be charged with murder. Viv and Jeff had been called and both were on their way to Lin's house.

Nicky sat in Leonard's lap getting patted and scratched. "Anyway, this little guy is the hero of the day. He found Amanda's body and he bit Robinson in the leg." The little dog rubbed his head against the man's chest.

Lin beamed at her sweet animal.

"How'd you figure out it was Robinson?" Leonard asked.

"I don't really know." Lin rubbed at her temple. "When I got the text from Viv telling me that Milliken had an alibi, my head felt like it was about to explode. All the little pieces about the cases were swirling in my brain. I got the idea to look up how Audrey Robinson died. As soon as I read the story online, I knew Ted killed her. Audrey must have suspected him or found out that he had something to do with Madeleine's disappearance. I bet she told Amanda her suspicions, so Amanda came to the island to try to find out more. Ted came to Nantucket to convince Amanda that Audrey was wrong about him. Amanda wouldn't listen to him so he strangled her. Then he killed Brian."

Leonard swallowed hard and shook his head. "Hard to believe a person could do such things."

"Should we even classify him as a person? A monster is more apt." Lin's eyelids drooped. "There's still quite a lot left for the police to figure out."

"Leave them to it. You did your part."

"Why'd you come back?" Lin crossed her arms on the table.

"I don't really know." Leonard ran his hand through his hair. For a man in his early sixties, he still had a full head of hair. "I was heading out to do an errand and the idea came into my head to come over and check on you. You didn't look so good when I left you here earlier. The front door was open a crack, so I came in. You don't look so good now, either."

Lin narrowed her eyes at him. "Thanks a lot."

A cool breeze ruffled Lin's hair and Sebastian Coffin materialized standing right behind Leonard. The ghost stood ramrod straight in his formal coat. He gave Lin the tiniest bow and looked at Leonard. The hint of a smile formed on Lin's face. She knew that Sebastian must have sent Leonard the idea that he ought to come over and see how she was doing.

"What are you lookin' at?" Leonard glanced over his shoulder into the darkness. "Is there a ghost standin' behind me or somethin'?"

Sebastian faded away.

Lin's smile broadened. "Yeah, there was."

Just then, Jeff rushed out of the house and onto the deck. He hurried to Lin and gathered her in his arms leaning his face into her hair. "Are you okay?" He ran his hand gently over her long, brown locks.

A police officer opened the screen door and poked his head out. "We're all set in here, Ms. Coffin. You and Mr. Reed will most likely be called to the station by the detectives in the next few days. Glad you're safe and sound." He gave Leonard a nod. "Nice work, Mr. Reed." He looked at Lin. "We'll let ourselves out."

"Where's my cousin?" Viv's voice could be heard in the living room. She brushed past the police officer and dashed onto the deck where Lin was still wrapped in Jeff's arms. "My God." Viv stood behind Lin and stretched her arms around her cousin and Jeff. "You're not supposed to get attacked unless I'm with you."

They all chuckled.

Leonard lifted Nicky off his lap and placed him on the deck. "I'm heading home."

Lin extracted herself from the two pairs of arms, walked over to Leonard, and hugged him, resting her head on his chest. "Thank you," she whispered.

When Lin stepped back from the man, Viv ran over and squeezed him in her arms. "You are a wonderful man."

Leonard's cheeks flushed pink. "Good night," he muttered and scooted into the house, crossed the living room, and went out the front door to his truck.

CHAPTER 25

"You want me to go with you?" Viv picked a piece of lint off of Lin's skirt.

Lin stood next to the upholstered chair where Nicky and Queenie were sitting. "I'm okay to go alone. Thanks for letting Nicky stay here while I'm gone. I'll be back by mid-afternoon."

Viv leaned against the beverage counter and crossed her arms over her chest. "I couldn't believe that Robinson buried Amanda just a few yards from where he buried Madeleine years ago. Who could even make this stuff up?"

"Yeah. The news article said that Robinson fell in love with Madeleine and when she repeatedly rebuffed him, he became enraged and strangled her. He buried her on the Milliken's farm. It was remote, private. He thought it was the perfect spot to hide the body."

Viv shook her head. "No one ever found Madeleine so Robinson buried Amanda there, too. His child. Good grief, I can't even fathom it." Her voice was weary. "You can't trust anyone," Viv declared.

"No one?" Lin eyed her.

"Well, a few people."

Lin hugged her cousin. "I'm just glad it's over. The girls can rest in peace."

"Have you seen them lately?" Viv whispered.

Lin shook her head and checked her watch. "I'd better get going."

Viv walked her cousin to the door of the bookstore. "Hurry back. Want to come over for dinner tonight? We haven't played guitar together for weeks. I'll invite the guys. We can make a fire outside and have a sing-along."

"Then you'll make me get up on stage and sing with your band again and mortify me." Lin stepped onto the sidewalk.

"Hmm." Viv tapped her finger to her chin. "I forgot about that." She gave her cousin a wicked grin.

***

LIN PARKED in the cemetery lot and followed the long line of mourners to the graveside where she saw Libby and Anton and went to stand beside them. The rims of Libby's eyes were red and she clutched a tissue in her hand. Anton had his arm around her shoulders. Lin glanced at the huge crowd. She couldn't believe that so many people had gathered for Liliana's burial.

"How old was she?" Lin asked Libby.

"Old."

"I wish I'd met her more than once."

"You were lucky," Libby said. "She took your hand."

Lin looked at Libby wondering what she meant. Before Lin could question her, she saw a man walking over to them. He was wearing pressed chinos and a white starched dress shirt with a blue tie. His hair was neatly combed.

Lin's eyebrows went up and she smiled at Leonard. "You look nice."

Leonard glanced down, embarrassed. "Liliana was a good person."

"You said you worked for her for years. Did you know much about her?" Lin kept her voice low.

"Next to nothing." Leonard gave a shrug. "Except that she was good and kind and helped people."

They stood quietly for a few minutes and then Lin leaned closer to Leonard. "You know, I've been thinking."

Leonard eyed her.

"After we met with Milliken the other day about his landscaping wants, I got to thinking about what he said. Would you have any interest in officially joining forces with me? I know I don't know much, but I learn pretty fast and...."

"What are you babbling about, Coffin?"

"How would you feel about forming a company

with me? Make it official. Maybe hire some people to work for us. We could write up a proposal for Milliken for the landscaping job he wants us to do and see if he accepts it." Lin bit her lip waiting for Leonard to say something.

Leonard turned to her and looked her in the eye.

Lin went on. "Over time, maybe we could invest in some equipment. Expand. People like our work. It might work out really well."

Leonard narrowed his eyes. "You want to start a company with me?"

"Yes?" Lin mumbled. She reached into her pocket. "I made a prototype." She handed Leonard a mock-up of a business card. It was a cream-colored card with the words, "L and L Landscaping and Gardening Services," their names and phone numbers, and the image of a flowering bush on it.

Leonard stared at the card for a long time. "Does the first 'L' stand for your name or mine?"

Lin smiled. "Is that a yes?"

"I think it is."

Lin grinned and high-fived Leonard.

A hearse and a black car pulled up beside the lawn where they were standing. A minister got out of the car and pallbearers carried the coffin to the prepared site. The crowd stepped closer as the minister read from the book of prayers that he held in his hands. A woman sang an acapella version of a favorite hymn of Liliana's and it was so sweetly beautiful that tears formed in Lin's eyes. When the short service was over, the minister invited the mourners to join together at Liliana's former home in 'Sconset for a buffet luncheon. As people began to slowly file away, a violinist and a cellist began to play.

A cool breeze blew over the assemblage and Lin shivered. Just as she was about to turn away, something caught her eye. Liliana's spirit stood next to the casket shimmering brighter than any ghost Lin had ever seen. Even though no one could see the ghost, Liliana smiled tenderly at the people gathered for her service.

Lin suddenly felt as if she'd stepped into a walk-in freezer and when she looked to the right behind Liliana, she nearly gasped. There must have been two hundred spirits waiting for the new ghost to join them. Liliana turned and walked slowly toward the spirits who parted in the middle so that she could walk between them. Each one nodded as the woman moved past and up the hill and they closed behind her and followed her as she made her way to the treeline.

Lin saw Sebastian Coffin and his wife Emily in the group. Three ghosts, two young women and a young man, stepped from the procession and looked back. The two girl ghosts could have been sisters. Madeleine, Amanda, and Brian smiled at Lin, then turned and joined the others as the hundreds of shimmering ghosts climbed the hill. They followed Liliana into the grove of trees and disappeared.

Out of the corner of her eye, Lin noticed Leonard staring at the hill. He caught her looking at him. "What? What's wrong with you?" he asked.

"Are you chilly by any chance?" Lin asked suspiciously.

"What?" Leonard's voice sounded nervous.

"Why do you sound so nervous?" Lin narrowed her eyes. "You see a ghost or something?"

A corner of the man's mouth went up. "No such thing as ghosts, Coffin. Come on. Let's go get some lunch."

The new business partners followed Libby and Anton down the hill to the cars, the summer air cool and sweet and the sun shining down on them.

THANK YOU FOR READING!

BOOKS BY J.A. WHITING CAN BE FOUND HERE:

www.amazon.com/author/jawhiting

To hear about new books and book sales, please sign up for my mailing list at:

www.jawhitingbooks.com

Your email will never be sold, shared, or spammed.

BOOKS BY J. A. WHITING

LIN COFFIN COZY MYSTERIES

A Haunted Murder (A Lin Coffin Cozy Mystery Book 1)
A Haunted Disappearance (A Lin Coffin Cozy Mystery Book 2)
And more to come!

SWEET COVE COZY MYSTERIES

The Sweet Dreams Bake Shop (Sweet Cove Cozy Mystery Book 1)
Murder So Sweet (Sweet Cove Cozy Mystery Book 2)
Sweet Secrets (Sweet Cove Cozy Mystery Book 3)
Sweet Deceit (Sweet Cove Cozy Mystery Book 4)
Sweetness and Light (Sweet Cove Cozy Mystery Book 5)
Home Sweet Home (Sweet Cove Cozy Mystery Book 6)
And more to come!

OLIVIA MILLER MYSTERIES

The Killings (Olivia Miller Mystery Book 1)
Red Julie (Olivia Miller Mystery Book 2)
The Stone of Sadness (Olivia Miller Mystery Book 3)

If you enjoyed the book, please consider leaving a review.

A few words are all that's needed.

It would be very much appreciated.

ABOUT THE AUTHOR

J.A. Whiting lives with her family in New England. Whiting loves reading and writing mystery, suspense and thriller stories.

VISIT ME AT:

www.jawhitingbooks.com

www.facebook.com/jawhitingauthor

www.amazon.com/author/jawhiting

Made in the USA
Middletown, DE
22 August 2016